Prologue

Jonathan Mcdell was a mad man . He was so worked up and fixated on his work, that he would spend hours in his laboratory . He would sit at his desk as he mixed up chemicals , and solve unexplainable equations that no prodigy or Einstein could solve. He never left his office. He would be trapped in there for hours past the calls of his supper awaiting on the table. In his final days of life he dreamed of changing humanity . He wanted to be rich and famous and well known all across the world. He dreamed about this so much that he was too anxious to ever fall asleep . A nice Hot cup of Tea would soothe him , or a hot bath with bubbles might do the trick , but he just couldn't fall asleep . On One cold dreadful December morning at around christmas time ,   Jonathan began to map out his evilest and most scorchingly plan that would soon destroy the world's capability . He smiled mockingly as he admired his lifetime's work . Never had he dreamed up something so magnificent in his 75 years of life . He began to mix potions together in a large boiling cauldron that would eventually vaporize the toxic room . He made mental calculations in his head as he went . His hands did the work. His hands were like a magicians . Smooth and quicker than the blink of an eye. Adrenaline began to kick in as the hours of morning began to fade to the darkness of night .His sharpest lab coat was splattered with chemicals, his face was red and damped with sweat. A long day of hard work was starting to take a toll on him. After 20 hours of nonstop work his greatest invention was coming to an end . The calculations began to add up, the chemicals began to mix, and the potion was begging to stir. Soon his project would be finished . It was only a matter of time , until the whole world would know his name.

Chapter 1 : The worst summer ever

Connor Davidson was not enjoying his summer break . Filled with boredom and misery, he just couldn't find anything fun to do. He spent his weekends binge watching netflix shows, and playing super mario bros on his switch . He hated being self isolated in his bedroom. He wanted something spectacularly to happen in his life that for once would make him happy . He wanted to do so much more than live a boring life. But he knew that that was a long way ahead of him. On day One Hundred and Six of quarantine he started dropping pennies in a jar. He would tallie his walls, and count down the days before he could get out of his prison cell and step into the outside world. Of course he couldnt do anything that stupid. His father was a doctor and knew better than him. Safety was the first priority. He would make sure his son always washed his hands with soap and water ,and that he didn't leave the house without a face covering. Connor hated this lifestyle , but he had to keep moving on and couldn't keep dwelling on the past, no matter how hard the truth hurt . On this particular day Connor felt light headed. He felt nauseous and found himself vomiting in the middle of the night. His stomach wasn't much better, and spent half of the morning locked in the bathroom . When he came down for breakfast he couldn't find himself hungry . He ate only a portion of his bagel, and only managed to take one bite of his cereal. He didn't even bother to touch his toast. After another week went by his mother had enough . She went shopping to the local pharmacy , where she picked up a prescription of medication . After arriving home on a late sunday morning with a box of frosted donuts from the local bakery and the medication in her hand, she ran to her son's assistance . She tried to feed her son a spoonful of ibuprofen . But Connor would put on a fight and wouldn't come to his senses to swallow the icky gooey substance. He hated the smell , and couldn't bear to get near it . He would stiffen up his nose like a baby not happy about green beans on his plate.

" Connor , the only way you're going to get better is if you take your medicine ," Mrs. Davidson insisted .

Connor rolled his eyes up. " I don't want to take it," he speculated. " It doesn't smell good."

Susan Davidson was beginning to get annoyed . She couldn't win.

" You're making this harder than it has to be, young man   . You have a whooping cough, a stomach ache, and a highly severe fever ."

" Im okay ," Connor pleaded. " Really, I am fine."

" You are not ok ! You have a virus that has killed millions of lives , and I don't want you to spread it . You've seen what this sickness has done to our family ."

Connor felt a sense of guilt. He recalled the death of his uncle just a week past , and his sick grandmother who was on her deathbed, soon to be recalled dead.

" I haven't thought about it that way ," Connor said apologetically. " I hadn't really considered how much it has wrecked our family," He stared into his mothers crystal clear blue eyes.

Mrs. Davidson sighed .

" I know this has been hard on you honey, I really do . I wish there was some cure to all of this ," she took another breath . " You know …. To make all of this go away ."

Connor bit back a smile.

" Sometimes I wish this would all go away too . Sometimes I close my eyes and hope tomorrow will be a better day."

" I know Connor , I sometimes wish that too," she said gazingly, staring off into space ." But we all have to stay strong and hope for the best ."

" Why do you do it ? " Connor questioned .

" Do what ?" Mrs. Davidson answered .

" Risk your lives, help people , don't you care about ever getting sick or putting yourself into harm's way? "

Mrs. Davidson chuckled . " That's a good question," she said looking upon her son . "But the main reason why me and your father do it is not because of the money … But because we want to help the people in need .

We want to make sure they're safe, and that they are put into the best care possible."

" But don't you know it's dangerous? Do you know the risk ? "

" Of course we know the risk , but that doesn't stop us from doing what's right . We want the best for everyone out there .. and to do that we have to face the risks and put ourselves in danger," Mrs. Davidsons said happily .

Connor looked up upon his mother. He saw more than just a mom, he saw a superhero. He saw a brave hero fighting for her life to prove society wrong. He saw justice, hope, and responsibility. He saw himself in her.

" You think you're ready for your medicine now ? " Connor's mother said .

Connor took a deep breath. " Why not ? how bad can it possibly be ?"

....

His plan had worked. Deaths were starting to rise, cases were going up, and the world was slowly getting weaker everyday . The man had nothing yet to smile than to the satisfaction of his domain . He knew the world was falling in his devious trap . He was the cat, they were the mouse. They were falling into the bait and he was getting stronger day by day. He managed to kill over millions of lives, and spread his disease across the world like a snap in the fingers . He knew soon the world would fall apart and he would be the all mighty ruler . Jonathan Mcdell never failed. He always won. Play him in cards and he would bring home the jackspot, play him in a game of chess and he would leave you in check mate. His plan was growing , and he could feel his victory coming closer . On one particular day Jonathan attempted to leave his lab for the first time in over a decade . He forgot how fresh air smelt, and how the beautiful charms of bird calls sounded like . He was scared at first, but then got used to the area around him . There was silence. It was peaceful. He could finally relax for once, and not be anxious and overwhelmed by the real world. The streets were deserted . Only 5 people were to be spotted. He was the only second individual to walk among overlapping roads. Jonathan strolled past an Irish bakery where the scent of vanilla and chocolate bean filled the old man's nostrils. He then hopped by an old toy shop that was filled with shelves of old fashioned teddy bears and rubber toy dolls . The man then galloped through a quite empty parking lot where a man was walking his labrador dog. It didn't look friendly and gave him the devil's eye. Jonathan took this as an insult ,but continued to mind his business . He was then on his way past Humphrey lane . The man checked his watch carefully, making sure he was not late for his private meeting . 12:30 , he was on time. The meeting didn't start until another 15 minutes. Tick! tick ! The clock chimed as his shoes were beaten lightly against the coopings of the thick dry cement . He tried not to stand out , but only wished to proceed to his destination .He stopped at an intersection. He waited for the green light, then it was his que to go. He tipped his hat and began his usual route towards 341 North Secura Avenue . After a long man's hike , he arrived at his destination. An old rundown house that was shaped like a triangle , and bent at a 90 degree angle . The windows were unmarkingly shattered and dented and looked like they were destroyed by baseballs . The house looked vacant , except for a man sucking a cigarette on the front porch. He was agging pretty well, with fine gray hair and wrinkly skin. He looked around 75 years old. He was wearing a polo Hawaiian t-shirt and short cuff jeans down to his knees. You could tell he was a chain smoker. His teeth were sticking out, they were rotting from plague . He had not brushed his teeth for a decent 20 years , and you could see his chompers forming into the color yellow. You could smell his breath from a distance away. It smelled like spoilt milk and dirty socks.

" Excuse me sir, are you Randy Goss ?" asked the man politely .

The old man got up from his rocking chair. " I wasn't expecting any visitors at this hour ," the man replied. " You're 15 minutes early. The man spoke in a southern accent, Like he came from the midwest . His accent was noticeable.

" Yes, I'm really sorry . I left the building a little earlier so I could arrive on time ," Jonathan said . Jonathan stared at the man as he lit up another cigarette ." Do we still have the deal ? "

Mr. Gross puffed out the smoke. He was like a dragon breathing out fire.

" The deal ?" he asked ,like he never heard of any negotiating business they had discussed in the past.

" Don't you remember ? Last week we talked on the phone . We discussed how if I gave you some cash you would give me the suit . Does that ring any bells ? " Jonathan asked.

" I now seem to recall that ," coughed the old man. "But i can't make the deal without a bargain."

" How much do you want ? "

The man seemed to give this thought.

" 10 million," he decided . "Final answer ,I ain't doing anything lower than that ."

Jonathan's face lit up in surprise .

" 10 million !! Are you out of your mind? Do you know That's a crazy amount of money you're offering !"

The boss chuckled. " That's the policy, look i make the rules here if you can't afford it just forget about it ."

Jonathan cursed to himself. There had to be another way .

John fumbled through his wallet , All he had on him was Five One-Hundred dollar bills and 4 silver quarters. He wasn't going to get paid for another 3 weeks . He was not sure how he was going to make this bargain work .

" I'm sorry ,but all I have is 500 bucks and a few quarters ," Jonathan informed .

The Boss slammed his fist onto his rocking chair. Jonathan flinched.

" Didn't I tell you before ," he pointed his crooked finger."No less than my bragian then no deal."

Jonathan Mcdell had to be careful. If he didn't give his boss what he wanted , he would be shot in the back of the head.

" I only make 7 million a year ," Jonathan exclaimed ." I Am rich indeed but what you are telling me to receive is way past my fortune ."

" Don't inform me about your struggles , Jonathan. Don't you know how much my company has struggled in the past 40 years ?" the man settled himself back down in his rocking chair." If you don't have the cash then get out of my property and don't you dare... Ever think of coming back !"

Jonathan zipped up his coat , and walked away from the rundown structure . In this case he didn't even worry about saying goodbye .On his way home, he came across an idea. A crazy idea! The only way to get the money he thought to himself , was to rob the local county bank. He smiled to himself with pleasure. Then it was settled, next Tuesday he would rob the bank just East of Division. He may kill hundreds of people in the process, but at least he was going to make the deal of his life.

Chapter 2 : The visit

Connor was beginning to feel better . His stomach pain went away, and his cough was unnoticeable . He felt much better than the last couple of days , and wasn't that run down and fatigued. He had more energy , and was starting to act like his normal self . His diet was back to normal. He wasn't stuck eating and drinking the occasional soup and ginger oil. He was now eating 2 cheese burgers a day , and lots of vanilla fudge ice cream. He was more active and put a lot of sugar in his system. His mother would have to settle him down at 9, or he would be bouncing off the walls all night. One morning, when Connor was still lying around in bed, the voice of his father startled him awake. The voice was an echo, loud and clear .

" Connor, are you awake ? It's nearly 20 past 10 ."

Connor bolted his head up from under the covers. He rubbed his eyes.

" I must have overslept."

Connors father gleamed at his watch .

" Yeep ... You sure did . Didn't we talk about this ? You're supposed to be in bed at a reasonable hour . You can't keep staying up all night ."

Connor scratched his head.

" It's summer break Dad , " Connor said stubbornly . "I don't go to school till August .Besides, all my friends stay up late , why can't i?"

" Because ," said Connor's father. "This is bad hygiene. I don't want my son under the influence of staying up late and partying," Mr. Davidson said in concern.

" But Dad, you always tell me that when you were younger you did the same thing . You partied on weekends, and pulled all-nighters . Why can't I do it too? " Connor asked curiously .

" That was a long time ago. I was young and stupid, I didnt no better. I made a mistake ! And do you know what it led to ?"

Connor didn't speak a word. He laid there in disapproval.

"It led to me failing my exams, and disappointing my parents . It led to broken shattered dreams . My parents always had faith in me . They wanted me to do good in school and not be a bum on the streets. They wanted the best of me, and sometimes the best had to be being better than everybody else. I almost gave up, I was sent to a rehab facility . I didn't want to live any longer. I wanted to kill myself. But then 2 years later I got back up on my feet. I had another go. I made sure I stayed on task and did my homework. I then got offered a scholarship to a university. And became a doctor . My dream, my parents' dream, had come true . Just don't mess up like I almost did son . Think smart and be assertive." Connor nodded his head. He was surprised. He had never known his father went through any of this . He did not know how much his father sacrificed in his life . He always thought of him as a child who lived a nice life, and grew up so magnificently . But lying there in his bed, he knew his father wanted the best of him, and did not want his son to go through the chaos he overcame .

" Any way ," Mr. Davidson said, changing the subject. " Why don't you get dressed and we hit the road."

Connor smiled. Maybe his dad would take him out to chucky cheese, or he would go to an amusement park. He couldn't hold in his excitement.

" Where to ?"

Connors father lowered his expression .

" We have to go visit your grandmother ... She's been going through a lot these past couple of months . I promised your mother we would check on her."

Connors expression lowered . He hated visiting his grandmother. He hated having to see her suffer and see her not well.

" Oh,"Connor said, clearly disappointed. " I thought we were going to have a father and son day ? You know .. Do something fun."

The man by his bedside frowned.

" I wish that too. But this is very important. We haven't seen Memaw for over a month."

" I just hate going there . It makes me so heartbroken to see her in such a bad stage in her life," Connor exclaimed .

"Well, I know from my experiences how hard it is."

" You do ?" Connor said as he looked his father in the eyes .

"Of course," Mr. Davidson proclaimed. " Do you know how hard it was for me to see my great grandmother on her deathbed? Every day she would get sick and weaker. She was suffering from dementia and didn't even know my name for the last 5 years of her life ," Mr. Davidson wiped a tear from his cheek, it was hard for him to proceed on. So he took 2 long mellow deep breaths. " I stood by her the day she died. I remember how she looked up at me and said " Goodbye." I remember the funeral like it was yesterday. Crows chirping a sad song , unknown figures of the party in black and white trench coats'."

Mr. Davidson looked into the eyes of his son. " I know it's been hard on you . You're only a kid. The world is evolving around you . And it's ok to be scared. We're all scared at times. But sometimes you have to face your fears. Face the darkness , or the devil , or the unknown. You have to confront it ."

Connor took a long deep breath .

" I'm sorry you went through all of that ."

" No need to apologize . You didn't do anything wrong. That's just how life works. Life isn't perfect, it's like a curveball. It's wild, and it can knock you off your feet. But you have to stay strong , even though you feel like giving up," Mr. Davidson smiled . " Just remember that."

" I'll never forget anything you said dad ... I promise ," Connor swore.

....

Before they knew it they were up and about . They arrived at the hospital a little after 12 just in time for visiting hours. The father and son walked Into the main entrance of the building , where they could see a elderly thin lady working at the reception desk. She wore a long blue jumper , and was typing away on her laptop. She had short frizzy hair and was sucking a peppermint. Files and papers were overflooded on her desk.

" Excuse me ma'am ," Blurted out Mr. Davidson , walking up to the front desk. " I am here with my son to visit my mother ."

The receptionist looked up at the two patients.

" Last name ?"

" Davidson ."

The lady typed away on her computer.

" Marry Davidson ?"

"That's correct."

She stared at her computer screen.

"She will be in room 305 on the second floor."

" Thank you ."

" Oh, and you need to wear these."

The nurse handed out 2 paper masks.

" There's a virus going around," the receptionist said. " It's spreading fast and killing the economy. It's for safety procedures . So our patients don't get sick."

Connor and his father accepted .They pulled their masks over their mouths and nose. It was hard to breathe in. Connor felt like he would suffocate if he kept it on any longer.
Mr. Davidson and his son walked toward the elevator.   It was old and runned down, and had nothing more than 3 buttons labeled with the numbers 1 through 3 . The floorboards made creaky sounds , and it

wasn't the most comfortable to ride in . After a 30 second flight to the 2nd floor , Connor and his father began their walk toward room 305. Their hearts began to race , their palms were beginning to sweat, and they could hardly breathe in their suffocating masks . They passed different rooms labeled with different numbers, and saw nurses in the halls with large bags under their eyes . Connor knew how difficult it was to be a doctor . He knew about the crazy night shifts , and the nonstop working hours, and how it could really take a toll on you . He knew from his father that it wasn't an easy job . They continued down the narrow corridors. They turned on their left, and came across the room. They walked right in with no pleasure of knocking . In the corner of the room lies an elderly woman. She was thin and boney and you could tell she had been not eating . She was not in good shape.

" Hello mother ."

Connor followed in after his father . The room was dark and empty except for a vacant hospital bed that was on its last legs . The drapes were completely sealed and the only light came from the Tv in the room. Connor was scared, he never liked seeing his grandma in here. She acted very differently then how he remembered her all those years ago. Connor knew she only had only a few days left. But he just couldn't accept it. The idea of knowing that she wasn't going to be around.

 Mrs. Davidson and Connor made themselves comfortable in 2 vacant chairs.

" Do you remember me ? " Connor's father called out.

There was a moment of silence. You could see the confusion among the old woman's face.

" It's your son Mark, and your grandson Connor ."

The old women gazed into the eyes of the unknown trespassers. It was hard to make out every detail of her , she looked like a shadow.

" I don't know who you are ?" she questioned ." Matter of fact,I don't think I have a son or a grandchild ."

Connor was worried . He had never seen his grandmother in such a traumatic stage in her life . Slight tears began trickling down his face . He was getting scared.

Mr. Davidson started at the untouched food tray that lay on her bedside table. Clearly she hadn't touched her food and had no desire to bother taking a bite.

" Mom , why aren't you eating your food? You're not going to get out of this place if you don't eat ," Mr. Davidson exclaimed .

" I don't care for it ," the woman hollered. " I'm not hungry."

" Mom, you lost 25 pounds . You're underweight . The doctors give you three meals a day and you dont even touch it ."

" I don't like this place . Why did you send me here ? "

Mr. Davidson rolled his eyes up, and took the hand of his dying mother .

" Look, I know you don't like it here but it's for your own good. The reason you're here is so you can get stronger…….healthier, and be able to get back up on your feet . But if you decide to not do what's asked you're going to have to stay here longer ."

" No !" the woman howerd . " I want to go home . My husband is waiting . I have to feed the fish. I have to-."

Connor began to sob . His face was full of tears and he couldn't control his emotions . He wanted the screaming and the suffering to stop.

" Calm down ," Mr. Davidson interrupted." The doctors are taking good care of you . You don't have to worry about feeding the fish or anything like that. All you have to worry about is your health ."

The old women coughed. It was loud enough to startle two visitors.

" Do you have my car keys ? "

" Mom, we talked about this. You can't be driving anymore . You're way too old , and I don't want you to get in some car accident ."

“ I think it's in the garage .... Yes,” she assured. “ It must be there.”

Mr. Davidson had enough .

“ STOP IT !!!!” he roared in anger . “ YOUR NOT GETTING YOUR CAR BACK! , AND YOUR SURE NOT EVER GOING TO SEE YOUR HUSBAND EVER AGAIN,BECAUSE LET ME TELL YOU HE'S DEAD !!!! HE PASSED AWAY , HE AIN'T HERE NO MORE MA .... HE DIED WHEN I WAS 5, DON'T YOU REMEMBER ? ANSWER ME !!!! YOUR OUT OF YOUR MIND ! YOUR CRAZY !!!ARE YOU GOING TO FIX YOURSELF UP AND CONTINUE THIS CHAOTIC LIFE OR NOT ????? BECAUSE IF YOU DONT YOU MIGHT AS WELL END UP SUFFERING IN THIS DARK EMPTY ROOM .”

The man was lost for words . He could hardly catch his breath , and he could see the scared look on his child's face .He didn't like to see his son look so worried. It was the least thing any father liked to see , but he could not hold his emotions that lied inside him .As if on cue a nurse entered the room. She walked over to the dying womens bedside and injected her with some pills. The old lady then took a sip of water to wash it down. The nurse turned toward the 2 guests.

“ You must be visitors ,” the nurse pushed back a string of hair. She had a kind gentle smile.

“ Yes , that would be us ,” Connor's dad replied , trying to act calm.

“ Well, I just want to inform you about your mother,” the nurse couldn't see the patient's eyes. “ I have some bad news .”

“ What is it ? it isn't too serious is it ? “ Connor asked curiously , chiming into the conversion .

The nurse took a long deep breath, Like blowing a huge cake with birthday candles.

“ Well, we did some test results and found out your mother was diagnosed with brain cancer. I know it's a lot to process, but we're trying to do everything possible .”

Connor had a worried look on his face .His heart felt like a huge brick.

" Well, is there a cure? there has to be something you can do to save her right ?" Connor pleaded. He swallowed the huge lump in his throat.

" I am afraid not ." The nurse shook her head. " The doctors in our lab have tried to come up with something , but there seems to be no correct formula." She stared apologetically into the boy's eyes. " I'm sorry. And to you Mr. Davidson as well. I send my best regards."

" So that's why her memory isn't working ," Mr. Davidson added to the conversation .

The nurse nodded her head.

" Correct . She also suffers from severe dementia and that's why she's been acting strange lately ."

Connor wiped a tear from his eye . He was angry , and disappointed.

" How long does she have left to live ?" Connor trembled .

" About 3 weeks ."

Connor and his father gasped in disbelief.

" 3 weeks," Connor fumed. " That's it ?"

Mr. Davidson stepped in.

" Doctor , this must be a mistake ."

The nurse took a breath.

" I'm afraid not ."

....

It was around 7:45 in the morning . The sun was just rising, and the local whereabouts were off and about there days off to work. Local diners and shops were opening, and the newspaper boys were delivering the morning paper. Of course there was nothing interesting these days, just the same old politicians and that garbage. The only things that never seemed to get old were the updates on the global virus. People were getting sick of the mandates and rules, especially the Davidsons . On this particular day

Connor was eating a bowl of cheerios , with a side glass of freshly squeezed orange juice. One of his favorite ways to start the morning . His father sat right across from him, drinking his morning cup of brewed coffee and reading the daily paper. Susan Davidson was busy in the kitchen, making scrambled eggs and her homemade blueberry pancakes. Connor was tired. He had bags under his eyes , and he looked drowsy. He didn't get that much sleep the previous night. He was stressed , worried, and worn out. Mrs. Davidson noticed his behavior immediately.

"Are you ok Connor ? You look really tired."

Connors face was hidden behind a hoodie. Whatever he was trying to hide, wouldn't get past his mother.

" Connor, can you please take off the damn hood and answer me ?"

Silence.

Mrs. Davidson looked at her husband apologetically. Ongoing him to do something.

" Is it about grandma ?" Mrs. Davidson questioned .

Connor remained silent .

" Young man, why are you giving me attitude? I want to know what's wrong ".

Connor got up from the table. He knocked over his stool, and threw over the table. There was gasp and scream that skidded across the kitchen, as piles of food and hot beverages splattered to the floor. The kitchen was a mess. Syrup was everywhere,   and cups were broken in half.

" Look at me," Connor rasped . He took off his hood.

" See these scars . I tried to hurt myself ok ? I Am Depressed ." Connor put his head in his hands. " I don't want to live this stupid life. Nobody loves me, nobody cares about me . Grandmas dying for god sakes. And nobody is doing anything about it. And dont give me one of your stupid lectures and tell me everything is going to be ok. Because It's not". Connor choked back tears. His breathing was not stable and it was hard to go on.

" Connor don't say that , we love you very - ."

" SHUT THE HELL UP !" Connor's eyes turned red . His blue pupils had disappeared completely .

" Don't you dare speak to your mother like that mister," Mr. Davidson growled.

" I can speak to her however I want, " Connor said savagely . Connor closed his fists. Wine glasses shattered, and china plates smashed to the ground. Connor wasn't in control. He felt like an evil force was taking hold of him. And he couldn't do anything about it. The yellow neon lights in the dining room began to flicker , and Connor's face was turning into a ball of flame.His fists were a distant flame of ablaze, and his body was begging to heat up . He felt so angry inside . So angry that he wanted to destroy everything in his path .Without thinking about what he was doing, Connor shoved his mom. He didn't know how it happened; he just remembered her falling to the ground,screaming.

The 46 year old woman was caught by surprise, as she fell to the ground .

" CONNOR ! WHAT HAS GOTTEN INTO YOU ," boomed his father .

Mrs. Davidson lay on the floor , howling in agony.

" I'm sorry ," Connor pleaded. " I - didn't mean to-."

" Sorry is not going to cut it !! look at this mess , the kitchen is destroyed, and your mother is injured !"

" I don't know what happened . That - that wasn't me ."

" GET HIM OUT OF HERE, MARK !!! I DON'T WANT TO SEE HIM FOR THE REST OF THE MORNING ," cried Mrs. Davidson .

Connor did not know what to say . Something weird was going on with his body. Something that he was not in control of . He felt so bad for the mess he had made , and how he had injured his mother . He wished he could say sorry, but it was too late .

" Go to your room young man ," Mr Davidson hollered.

" Dad please... ."

" GO- TO-YOUR - ROOM ." Mr. Davidson ordered, sounding out each word.

" I didn't mean to push her - My anger , it got out of control and -."

" NOW !!!!!!!!"

Connor bowed his head down. All he could do was follow his fathers orders. He crept up the long narrow staircase and went up to his room. He lay on his bed staring into space. He was bored. He counted sheep, he tried reading a book , but nothing seemed to work . A little after 5pm a tray of hot turkey, and mashed potatoes was slid under the door of Connor's room. Connor accepted it. He was hungry, he hadn't eaten since the outbreak at breakfast. When the day drew darker he decided to doodle in his coloring book, and play call of duty on his XBOX. He lost track of time. He could hardly tell if it was Monday or Tuesday. He kept thinking about what happened. How he pushed his mom and said those horrible things . He knew that wasn't him. He wasn't that kind of person. He didn't know how he broke the glasses , or how he made the room dark , but whatever happened wasn't him. Magic couldn't be real , that stuff was only in movies. His parents thought he was crazy, maybe they would send him away to a military camp. He hated the thought of it. You could say Connor was a troubled kid. He had had these experiences all of his life. He would get right ups at school from his teachers complaining about him.The truth was Connor was a good kid. He had it in him. But he couldn't control his anger. He was talking to a psychiatrist once a week and was prescribed medication. But today's behavior was past the definition of acceptable.

Chapter 3 : The robbery

 The Houston county bank was located in a small village, just north of Nassau bay . It was an old building that was over 100 years old, and was a quite residential place for ongoing villagers. People came in here for financial reasons as well as wellbeing reasons. You could deposit checks , talk to an assistant about your balance and checks, and get free lollipops on Sunday afternoons . Tonight the bank was hardly crowded, there were a few people in the lounge area but not that much staff . Of course it was a Monday night, and you wouldn't expect too good of a crowd. Due to the virus, thousands of workers were out of work, and were cooped up in their homes. At around midnight a man in a rubber mask with a 200k pistol entered the building. There was no security , which made it much easier for him to break in. When he entered the building he could see a receptionist sucking a mint and typing away on a keyboard. He looked around, there were only a few dozen people. He had to make this quick. Before anyone called the police. He had to find the vault, and get the cash. A few of the customers were startled by the wake of the man. A 5 year old was clutching onto her mother, and a 75 year old was already out the door. No one knew why he was here, but they knew he was up to no good. The man pulled out the gun, and pulled the trigger. The chandeliers on the polished ceiling exploded in a destruction of glass . Dust flew from the cardboard under the ceiling, people were shielding themselves for cover .

" EVERYBODY TO THE GROUND NOW !"

The pastors obeyed and followed his orders. They were startled and scared.

The man walked over to the receptionist.

" Where's the vault ? "

" I-I -I don't know,"she stammered clearly, alerted by the gun.

The man grabbed hold of the lady by the neck.

" You will tell me or I will shoot you in the back of the head, " he pointed the pistol at her scalp. " Understood ?"

" Yes- Yes I understand sir ." The women took a deep breath . She knew she was going to be fired from her job . But she would rather live than get killed. "The money is on the 3rd floor," she said , not giving a second thought.

" What's the code?" he begged .

" I don't know what the code is . I just work as a receptionist."
The robber slapped her on the cheek. Jonathan was clearly getting impatient .

" Don't play games with me you fool."

The woman was brought to tears. Her breathing was heavy, and she was in a stage of panic . She didn't want to die . She had a family, grandkids, and lived in a beautiful neighborhood . She wasn't ready to leave behind this world .

" Fine, I'll tell you ! Just ... just please don't hurt me ,ok ?" stammered the woman .

The man chuckled like he had just heard a joke. " Hurt you ? No, it's more simple than that . I'm going to kill you."

" Please sir , spare me."

" You want mercy , then you better tell me the code ."

" Ok . Give me a second ." The woman clicked away on her computer as she went through hundreds of files . She could feel the gun being pressed on her back. "It's 14567 ."

" Are you sure ? " the man questioned .

" Yes of course ! Why would I lie to you ?"

The man gave this thought ." I hope you won't contact the police young lady," He stepped closer to her. " Because if so I will kill you with no hesitation. Understood? "

" Yes , I understand ."

" Good, now hand me the key."

The woman took a breath .

" Alright, let me get it ," She said as she walked towards her desk and pulled out a silver thin key from a brown drawer .

" Give me that." The man snatched the key . He let go of his grip on the lady and shoved her aside .Jonathan Mcdell made his way down the long open hall. His gun was by his side, and he made his way towards a long spiral staircase. His black boots tapped against the metallic floor , and his palms were sweating . He only had 2 minutes before the police arrived, and 120 seconds before he would be caught red handed. He needed this money . He needed the suit so he could take over the world, and get his revenge . Hurrying past a women's restroom, and a dark empty office , The man finally had arrived on the 3rd floor. It was quiet and empty, and you could hear the sound of a clock tick back and forth in the distance . Computer screens, and chairs were empty , and no one could be found . Jonathan took a right, then a left, then another right , and soon enough had arrived in front of a large gray vault . The vault was locked . Jonathan taped the digits into the transmitter , and put the key in the lock. And Voilà the vault opened. There were millions of dollar bills stacked high , like a mountain. He was going to be rich. He could travel the world, go to expensive dinners and his most favorite part... serve his duty and become the head boss for his business. Time was running out. Three minutes before the police would arrive. The alarms screamed, red lights flashed. He cursed himself. That lady must have contacted the police without him knowing. He should have killed her when he had the chance. He took out a bag and started to dump the cash in. He shoved in everything he could fit. Then he made his way to a secret exit and got in a van. This was all staged. They had discussed the plan earlier. The Head driver Charles would pick up Jonathan right off 20 seconds street, no later than 2:45. Jhonathan hopped in the back sheet and dumped the cash in the trunk.

"Hit the wheel," Jonathan shouted.

Charles hit the gas , speeding at a range of 100 miles per hour. They sped through red lights , and intersections , almost killing everyone in their direction. Out of the rearview mirror Jonathan spotted a cop car right behind their tail.
" Go faster, " Jonathan demanded . " The cops are on our lead ." The van picked up speed and turned left off of harlem. The police siren wailed though the streets , its red and neon lights flashing. 3 back up squad cars followed . " Good damn it ," Jonathan yelled. " We're never going to get away." Jhonatan reached over to the back seat and produced a gun. He took aim and fired 3 bullets at the windshield. Exploding glass came hurtling down. One squad member was hit right in the head. The officer fainted and the squad car began to lose control. It ran into other cars causing screaming and panic. The car hit shops and buildings , destroying everything in its path. As the two remaining cop cars soared through Harlem street , they were left shocked to find a huge fire and a group of screaming people.   They were confused and didn't know what had happened. All they knew for sure was that John Mcdowell had escaped once again.

···

The old man was waiting peacefully. His arms stretched out, and his feet supported him on a brown pillow. A brown cigarette was hanging from his mouth, and a glass of champagne was classified beside him . His house was a mess. Bills, checks, cash, and dozens of beer bottles were scattered everywhere . A white tabby cat was playing with a mouse, and a run down television set was playing in the distance . Just after another sip of red wine, the sound of the doorbell sprang across the room.The man was startled, and did not know who was at the door. He got up from the couch and opened the door. He was surprised who he saw. It was Jonathan .

" Jhona ?"

Jonathan shat down on a nearby stool. He seemed to be out of breath.

" Would you like a glass of water? " the old man offered.

Jonathan nodded politely. The man got a glass from the cabinet and filled it with sink water. He handed it over to John.

" Do you have the money?"

" Yes."Jhonathan took the glass and brought it to his lips. The water was cold and refreshing .

" Where is it?"

Jhonathan set the glass down and handed him over a brown leather bag. The old man blew out a ring of smoke and poured out the cash onto the kitchen counter. He counted to himself, all the stack of bills. . Perfect! His assistant had done the job and had brought him the cash. He was proud.

" Seems like you have done me your duty ," the old man replied .

" Yes sir."

" You have been a great assistant , and it has been a pleasure working with you , " the old man replied, swinging a shoulder over Jonathan ." You gave me what I wanted so I perhaps should give you what you signed up for ."
Jonathan smiled proudly. The old man, slicked his mustache, and led the way to a brown cellar door. It was old, and there were large carvings dented across the hedges . Jonathan was hesitant at first, not knowing what lay inside the cellar. Spiders ? Cobwebs? Mice? The most terrifying thoughts bloomed into the maniac's head, as he made his way down the creaky wooden stairs. The old man flashed on his flashlight and light beamed across the darkness. It was chilly down there. It felt below 20, and the heat was broken down. The stairs were rusty so they had to be careful walking down. The unknown shadows were lurking mysteriously, it was so dark you couldn't tell if it was night or day. There may even have been ghosts down here. Every time you proceed on you could feel like someone was behind you. Watching you. Almost like a six sense.

" Here we are ," the old man crooned . In the corner of the room there laid a large glass structure. The glass was sustainable, and inside there laid a large metal robotic suite .Jhonathan was too stunned to speak. He was lost for words. It was the most extraordinary thing Jonathan had ever seen .

" Want to try it on?" the old man questioned.

 Jonathan walked up to the glass .

" Yes, please. Thank you so much for this amazing opportunity ."

The old man smiled .

" My pleasure . You give me what I want , and I give you what you want, that's how deals work ."

Jonathan nodded. The old man fished a key from his pocket, and threw it to jonathan.

" Here you go. The bathroom should be in the back . . .. hope it fits."

Chapter 4 : The invitation

Connor awoke to the sound of pounding on his bedroom door. He turned around in his bed trying to get comfortable, but too many things were on his mind . On the 5th knock Connor had enough . He leaped off his bed , and turned the knob.

" You got something in the mail."

To Connors suspicion, his father was standing in the doorway .

" For me ?" Connor clarified .

Mr. Davidson looked his son in the eyes .

" I would suppose it is because it has your name on it ."

Connor was still confused. He never got any gifts or letters from anyone.

" Umm…. Well ok, where's it from ? " Connor asked .

Mr. Davidson peered through his spectacles on the back of the envelope.

" Some place called The Heroes academy … Whatever that is ," He chuckled.

Connor accepted the envelope from his father , and slammed the door .

  " I wonder who would send this to me? " Connor whispered under his breath .

Connor excitedly wrapped open the envelope and found a card with cursive handwriting . It had a paragraph of large text, and was neatly folded . Connor unfolded the piece of parchment and gazed at the letter .

To: Connor Davidson

If you have stumbled across this letter then congratulations ! You, as well as many other significant children will be invited to stay at my all new superhero academy !   Our first training lesson will be held on sunday, June 14th . Lessons will go on throughout the summer, and kids will be provided with dorm rooms and free meals . The directors will also be providing everyone with superhero suits, and gear for your upcoming missions Please make sure to bring gym shoes, clean clothing, and anything else for your comfort . This afternoon I will come to pick you up , and provide you with transportation . Please keep in mind that no one should know where you're going. If anyone ever finds out about your superhero powers and my academy, I'm afraid things will not end pleasantly . Once Again If you have any further questions or concerts feel free to report them to your head director.

Thank you !

Sincerely : Dr. sanchez

Connor glanced back at his watch . It was only 2:00 pm , and he had about 45 minutes to kill . He sat on his bed and thought of a plan. He knew he was grounded , and would spend the rest of his summer vacation locked up in his room. At the back of his mind he understood that it would be hard to get past his parents, but he knew he had to do something . Connor always wanted to have the opportunity to do something amazing in his life . He was getting bored of being stuck in the house for the past year, and he was ready for an adventure . A BIG one!

30 minutes later Connor was getting ready for his departure . He packed his bags with toiletry , his toothbrush, clothing , and his other belongings he would need. Connor tried not to pack too many things , but by the end of the afternoon he had 3 full suitcases worth of belongings ! Connor took a few deep breaths and gazed out the window . It was already a little past 2:45 and there still was no sign of anybody . Maybe the director was late or maybe he wasn't coming. Connor felt a sense of remorse due to the fact that his parents were out for lunch. This would be a perfect time to make a death defying escape and run away. Just before he was about to give up, a large blue and black vehicle sped down the road . It roared across the quiet streets and startled Connor by surprise . In the passenger seat a handsome man with a large blue cape and a red jumper could be seen . He looked himself in the mirror and then stepped out of the vehicle . His boots skidded across the pavement as he made his way towards Connors home . Connor opened his bedroom window and made his way down. Connor took each step carefully being careful not to step on any loose breaks or ivy . If he fell from here he would easily break his leg or neck, and that wouldn't end well. Connor threw his luggage onto the pavement and took each step one at a time. When he was about 1 foot from the ground Connor leaped down and came spurling towards the concrete . He dusted off his pants and shirt and made his way towards the stranger. Connors first thought was that he looked like someone at a cosplay convention, by the way he was dressed.   The handsome man walked towards Connor with his hands on his hips . He had a bright smile that reflected against the sun, and large bulky shoulders. He looked a little bit younger than 30 , and had pimply cheeks . Connor could tell that this was definitely Dr. Sanchez.

" Well hello young fellow, you must be Connor Davidson ," the man said.

" Yep, that's me ."

The man observed the boy carefully. He surely didn't look like a superhero.He looked skinnier than a bowl of pasta.

"You got my letter, am I correct ?"

"Yes , but I'm not a hundred percent percent sure what it was clarifying ."

The man let out a laugh .

"Well I'm not really sure how to explain this to you, but all I can really say is that...... you're a superhero . I've been investigating you for the past couple of years and I have to say you really do have some great potential ."

"Wait,wait, wait ," Connor said. " Just to clear things up. You're saying that I am a superhero ? "

"That is correct ! "

Connor could not believe this, he felt like he was living in a dream !

"But that can't be true. Superheroes are made up. They are only in comic books and movies , but there is no such thing as a real one ."

"I know it may be hard to believe but I am telling you the honest truth . Ever since you were a baby, though you may not know it, you have been born with the capability to do amazing things. Today for example, during breakfast you were able to break glass, and almost caused a fire ! I mean, what other explanation is there?" Connor had to agree with the man. All his life he had these incidents he couldn't explain. He was given a gift that someone dreamt of having .

"Can I turn invisible? " a grin spread across Connor's face. "Can I fly ? Was I bitten by a radioactive spider? "

"Shhh... Must you keep your mouth quiet ." A elderly couple walked past them giving them a strange look. Dr. Sanchez held out his hand . " I know you have a million questions and I will answer them , but not now. People may be listening. I'll tell you all you want to know once we reach the academy.Now come on. You don't want to be late on your first day ." Dr Sanchez took Connors luggage and dropped it in the trunk. Connor then stepped into the car, and the man took the wheel.

" Nice ride, " Connor called from the back seat.

" Do you like it ? " Dr Sanchez glanced at Connor through the rearview mirror. " It's one of our newest models ."

" I was going to say it's like the batmobile ....You know from Batman ."

The man chuckled.

" The car is a lot like that. It can deflect bullets, reach high speeds , and even has a parachute launched in it ."

"Wow ! " Connor was too stunned to speak.

" Want to see how fast it goes ?"

" I don't think that's a good idea ," Connor called ." You see , I get carsick an-."

Before Connor could say more , the vehicle sped through the streets like a bullet reaching speeds up to 125 miles per hour.

" SLOW DOWN!" Connor protested .

Dr. Sanchez didn't seem to hear him.

....

The academy stood on a high deserted hill. It gleaned over the large pacific ocean, representing itself in a fashionable manner . There was a large black gate that covered the edges around the property, and statues of famous superheroes were displayed across the yard . In the distance a group of teenagers were soaring through the sky, and another group was shooting lasers out of their hands . Large billboards were surrounded across the outside walls , and counselors were seen giving instructions . The property was so big, it was like the distance of three football fields.

The school motto for the school was to try hard and succeed. No disappointment was encouraged as well as giving up. At the Heroes Academy you needed to be at your best. You needed to prove everybody you were the best without dignity or hesitation.

" WOW , look at this place !" Connor said , staring out the window.

" Amazing isn't it ? " Dr. Sanchez asked .

" Is this Hogwarts ?"

The man looked at Connor through the rearview mirror .He chuckled.

" No silly, this is nothing like Hogwarts . This academy is home to some of the greatest heroes that ever walked the earth ! This place is filled with tons of great instructors, and things beyond your wildest imagination."

" That's amazing ! Did Superman and Batman go here when they were kids?"

" Not on the record , but I can tell you that some of the most influential heroes' sons and daughters enrolled in the academy ."

Connors heart began to pound with adrenaline . He was so excited, he wanted to leap up with joy !

" You will be given a tour of the school and attend all your classes starting tomorrow morning ," the man informed.

Connor gulped .

" I'd love to have a tour . This place looks so amazing, I just can't wait to see what's inside ."

Dr. Sanchez pulled into the driveway .

" We're about to pull up... Make sure to grab your bag on the way out of the car, and follow my lead . I'd hate for you to get lost on your first day ."

The car came to a halt. Connor swung open the car door and grabbed his bags from the trunk. Doctor Sanchez helped carry the luggage and they proceeded up the gravel path. The 2 of them went up a large staircase , and opened a large set of double doors . There were over a dozen classrooms spreaded across the first level of the building . Lockers were covered on both sides of the walls, and a large cafeteria could be spotted to the right . The aroma of tasty foods and beverages could be scented across the hallways . Connors stomach churned , he hadn't eaten a big meal for a while and was starving . The 2 continued their walk through the first level , until Dr. Sanchez came to a sudden stop . A group of 3 young tenneagers could be seen standing against a large wall . There was 1 boy who was bulky and easily the size of a muscular football player , and 2 girls who seemed very joyful . They all had large smiles on their faces, and had their arms crossed.

" Connor, I'd like you to meet your tour guides. Their names are Frank, Jessica, and Sarah ," Dr. Sanchez explained as he pointed to the group of young heroes . "These younglings will be giving you a full tour of everything there is in this precious school. Please do not wander on your own and make sure to follow their instructions ."

Connor smiled, and nodded his head. His face turned red as he glanced at Sarah . She was a cute girl with long blonde hair, and a beautiful smile . Connor was starstruck . This was one of the prettiest girls he had ever seen.

 " Yeah of course . Whatever you say Dr. Sanchez ," Connor said, as he got back on topic .

The man smiled .

" Great ! then it's settled. Now remember tonight's dinner will be held in the main dining hall on the 4th floor . It's straight across from room B-38 ,but I'm sure these young fellows will be able to help you find it .. Again I hope you enjoy your tour and I look forward to seeing you later tonight ."

Chapter 5 : Old friends

John Mcdell was enjoying himself. He was drinking a bottle of scotch with an expensive new york stripe steak , which was served with a side of asparagus and baked potato. John was eating at one of the most expensive restaurants in the city, called Dans NightClub. Lots of celebrities and rich people would dine there and it was a pretty cmon place. Tonight , John was meeting with some of the executives of his corporation. They were going to have wine and discuss some business. Jonathan had a reason to celebrate . His deadly virus was spreading like crazy, and millions of people were in lockdown all across the country . It would only be a matter of time before humanity would come to an end, and Jonathan would take over the world ! Deep down in his heart Jonathan knew what he had to do. If he wanted this virus to continue he'd have to keep mixing chemicals. It may take him over a decade to do it, but he wasn't going to give up . Jonathan had the suit, he had the accessories, now all he needed to do was believe in himself .

" How's the plan going, Johny ?" one of the men at the table questioned .

Jonathan stopped cutting his meat .

" To be honest it's not going exactly as planned. But The cases are beginning to rise and I think before long everything will work out ."

The stranger took a sip of wine .

" What we need to do is keep making the toxins. We need to establish a chemical which will be more effective and more proficient ."

" That's exactly what I was thinking ! I think it's best we find something that will launch this deadly disease more efficiently and quicker ,"Jonathan exclaimed .

" The economy can't keep up. Schools are already closing and half of the world is quarantined. The only reason everything hasn't fallen down is because we are a little behind on our schedule. But I guarantee in a week or so , the whole world will go extinct and mankind will be gone as we know it ."

A stern expression slid across John's face.

" I can't wait any longer ! Do you understand how important this plan is to me ! " John pounded his fist on the table . "If these cases don't rise at all then we're out of business ! We need some sort of new ingredient that is stronger than the previous ones. Something that will kill people, and destroy the world . We can't keep sitting around and hope for the best ! it's our time to shine."

" Yes doctor I understand, we're trying our best to make this plan work out . Just give us a couple of more days and we should have a better and stronger antidote that will be unstoppable ."

" Don't TRY ," Jonathan clarified. "Make it happen, I am paying you over 2 million a year for this job . If you can't do what I am assigning you then you're finished ."

" We understand sir ," The man said nervously.

" Good ," Jonathan stated. " Tomorrow we will rebuild and start fresh. We already planted over thousands of neopixels across the world, and all we need to do is make more. "

" You got it boss, we will get straight back to work and hopefully continue to launch these antitoxins sometime in the next couple of weeks ."

Jonathan shook hands with the director and greeted him goodbye. They then departed and walked their separate ways.

Chapter 6: World Domination

100,000 cases had been reported in the last 24 hours . The streets were filled with soaring ambulances , screaming children, and panic . Everyone in the city of Chicago was locked up in their homes coughing non stop, and lying in their beds . Schools were beginning to shut, businesses were going out of business, and a deadly virus was beginning to spread like a wildfire . NBC news had a lot to say about the economy and the deadly impact it was causing . People had no choice except to believe what they were hearing !
   "This is a time of severe crisis, "a young man claimed in the local newspaper . " These times are harder than we could have ever imagined , but we need to have hope ." No one knew what had caused such a deadly disease , some people claimed it was from a domestic animal, while others claimed it was a new variant of the flu . Whatever the cause was , this virus was doing more harm than good . People made sure they washed their hands with extra soap and water, and only left the house if they were One Hundred Percent . People had no choice except to follow the strict guidelines that the government made . The medical industry was running low on beds as well as providing blankets. The stakes were higher and The economy was slowly reaching extinction and there was nothing more than fear and concern. The advantage of being back to normal was taken before the hearts of thousands , even millions. The global health industry was even planning on creating vaccines which would protect individuals from catching the deadly virus. But a cure for such a deadly variant was far from being produced .   Thousands of miles away from the marvelous city of chicago, Jonathan Mcdell and his crew of elite members were working in a nearby laboratory . The laboratory was located in a large warehouse and was named : Genius Headquarters. It was an old run down building where people in yellow jumpers with oxygen masks produced chemicals that were highly dangerous. The building had maximum security, with tall wire fences and guards patrolling in every direction. Jonathan had opened this facility over a decade ago , and since then thousands of chemical samples and products were produced . Many

workers in the past had been affected in the factory. Some had gone blind while others simply went insane. Nobody could step into the factory without being targeted face to face with a gun or setting off an alarm. Everything was carefully monitored thanks to the help of the 100 cameras plated all across the facility. On this particular evening Jonathan was in his main office with a group of workers from the lab. They all looked defeated . Every person in Genius Headquarters was required to work around the clock every single day of the week. No breaks were accepted , except for small lunch breaks that were only around 20 minutes . Jonathan was the head director of genius headquarters. He was the boss, and often made the big decisions . He opened the company when he was 25 years old, and since then he had been making over millions of dollars a year .

"Sir , the antidote is complete," one of the workers protested, starting the conversation .

 Jonathan turned around in his chair ,A grin appearing on his face. He had waited over long enough , and the time was here.

"Wonderful ! May I see the sample ?"

"Of course , anything for you Doctor," the worker exclaimed as he handed his boss a large veil that was filled with a greenish liquid .

Jonathan admired the veil holding it in a careful fashion . If he dropped the veil, exploding glass would hit the floor, and 1 week of work would be down the drain. He had to be very careful!   John looked closely at the particles with his clear framed spectacles. He observed the gooey substance with pure content, and watched the liquid separate and swirl .

"Add 4 ½ more grams of nioxpiels ," Jonathan ordered his occupant. " And everything should be perfect." The stranger bowed politely and made his way back to his work table. To be precise, Jonathan wasn't the kind of human being to make mistakes. He wanted everything to go his way , and he made it happen. He wasn't the type who waited until the last minute to do something. He did his homework and stayed on schedule. Nothing went past him, not even the smallest thing.

Chapter 7: A Day off

" Welcome to heroes academy, home of the heroes !" exclaimed Frank as he pointed across the large halls of the school .

" Here you will learn how to control your superhero abilities, and learn the true meaning of hard work and friendship."

Connors face lit up with joy .

" This academy is filled with hundreds of training centers, restaurants, and plenty of things to keep you occupied.... You will be assigned to a dorm room with one other student, and expected to go to your mandatory classes from 8:00 am to 4:00 pm ! " Jessica, a stylish red haired girl chimed in .

" What if I get lost ?"

Sarah chuckled, " it tends to happen once in a while ."

" Yeah, there's like quizzillion floors," Frank said exaggeratingly. "Speaking of that , remember when that dude went missing and wasn't found for like a week ."

" Shut up Frank ," Sarah murmured. " We all know that's a lie , and besides." Sarah looked into Connor's eyes. " Don't be so hard on the newbie."

" Ok, fine ," Frank said, holding his hands up in surrender. " I was just having a little fun ."

The group made their way past a winding staircase , and descended past a group of counselors .

" I think you're really going to enjoy it here, Connor . The teachers are amazing , and the lessons are really interesting," Sarah quoted .

" Well this place sure does look amazing . It's like I'm living some sort of fantasy story ."

Sarah let out a laugh , her bright smile reflecting across the hallway .

" I thought the same thing when I first arrived ! "

Connor put his hands deep in his pockets . " I still can't believe this has happened to me. All of a sudden I am living a boring miserable life, and the next thing you know I'm sent to a superhero academy."

" I know, right ?" Frank said . " Being a superhero isn't easy kiddo .You get knocked down , but you gotta take the punches and expect what the world gives you ", he slid his arm over Connors shoulder ." Though you may not be ready for full responsibility and saving the world, you have to accept that you're different . You were born to share your supernatural talents with the world and protect those in danger . That's why you're here, Connor. You're not just some ordinary boy anymore , you're the hero everyone is calling for ... Do you get what I'm saying ? "

Connor nodded his head in agreement .

" Will I ever go home again ?" Connor asked . Though he knew the answer deep down inside his heart that he never would return, he wanted to hear someone else say it.

Frank slicked back his hair, looking Connor deep in the eyes .

" I'm afraid not . Being a superhero is kind of like a full time job . You have to commit to it and you are left with no choice but to pursue this passion and succeed ."

" For how long ? " Connor asked curiously.

"Forever !"

45 minutes later Connor had traveled to all 100 floors of the school. His legs were burning with pain after all of the flights of stairs he had to go up . Connor was starstruck on how amazing the academy was. There were 20 indoor pools ,including all kinds of restaurants and cuisines , as well as gyms (to work out in) and training facilities. On Connors guided tour he had also met some of the staff and directors at the academy. The principal Mr. Anderson greeted Connor warmly and babled that he was happy that Connor was enrolled in the academy. Connor also met Mrs. Feline who was pretty fast and furious, and who seemed like the teacher who gave you homework on the weekends. Connor gave a lot of handshakes and said a lot of Sirs and mams. He wanted to be polite and show his best manners. By the time the tour was finished dinner was about to begin . Hundreds of students jammed the hallways as they lined up in front of the cafeteria . Some were shoving each other , while others were simply waiting patiently . The smell of boiling soup and mashed potatoes lingered across the hallway. Connor was so excited and could hardly wait for the big meal . He had heard earlier that the cafeteria served great foods and drinks, and had the best key lime pie . Connor was looking forward to talking to some new kids , and hopefully making a friend or two . Connor walked with his tray and carton of juice over to an open table. To his surprise Sarah , Frank and Jessica were there.

" Mind if I sit here ?" Connor asked .

Frank looked up at Connor taking a bite from his bread roll. " Of course ."

Connor sat down .

" The food looks ... wonderful ," Connor said, eyeballing his tray.

" You bet ! but get a load on this, on Fridays they serve spaghetti and meatballs, and sausage pizza ! Oow boy I'm dreaming of it right now,"Frank said .

"Frank ," Jessica hollered ." Your drooling ," She backed away an inch .

" Oow sorry," Frank said as he wiped his chin with his sweater . " You know how much I love food ."

" You're like a carnivore," Sarah chimed in ." I still can't believe last year you eated 12 hot dogs in under 6 minutes."

"What ?" Connor was blown away .

" Yeah kid ," Frank said heroically. " I beat Matt Stonie's all time record ."

" You mean that guy from youtube who eats like 20 hamburgers in one sitting ? "

" That's him alright ."

" Weren't you in the bathroom for like 2 hours? " Sarah affirmed as she laughed quietly .

Frank blushed .

" Umm, yeah but ... can we not talk about that,"Frank stammered .

Connor chuckled . Frank was such a goofball.

" Anyway ," Frank said as he tried to change the topic . " What do you guys want to do this afternoon? I mean classes don't start again until tomorrow, and we literally have the rest of the night off ."

Sarah, Jessica, and Connor shared looks with one another.

" What do you like to do for fun, Connor ? " Sarah asked curiously .

Connor took a bite of his mashed potatoes and was quiet for a moment .

" Well, I'm a huge fan of video games . But I also enjoy swimming and reading books ."

" That's cool , as you just saw earlier Heroes Academy has a great library section , and tons of swimming pools ," Jessica chimed in . " I think you're really going to find a lot of things to do here , Connor ."

A proud smile gleamed across Connors face. He really was loving this place so far, and he knew he would have greater experiences in the coming years ahead .

" I guess we could all go make a trip to the swimming pool . Besides todays a really hot day and I think we all need to cool off," Sarah blurted .

The group all shook their heads in agreement. They could all use a nice break for a change .

" Yeah, sounds wonderful ! Once we are finished with supper we can all get changed and meet up on the 20th floor pool ," Sarah commented.

Connor put a hand on his head .

" Why do we have to go to the 20th floor ? I mean ,isn't there a swimming pool here on the first floor ?" Connor asked . He was clearly tired of walking up more flights of stairs .

" Because - " Sarah began . " The pool on the 20th floor is one of the best pools in the entire academy ! It has diving boards, a whirlpool, and a water slide ! The other pools don't have it .... Trust me you don't want to miss out ."

" Sounds amazing ! I'll bring some extra money if we all want to buy some smoothies and snacks after," Connor suggested .

Frank finally looked up from his cup of soup. His face was covered with chicken and rice and his cup was halfway finished .

" Did someone say smoothies ?" he asked proudly .

The group shared a laugh .

" Are you ever going to stop eating ? You literally ate 3 burritos for breakfast, 6 cups of chicken and rice soup , and now you want a smoothie? " Sarah asked sarcastically .

" I told you.... I love food ."

....

Connor went to his dorm room and quickly changed . He brought some extra towels and another set of clothes. Connor then made his way to the 20th floor pool where he saw Sarah and Jessica dressed in bikinis splashing around in the whirlpool, and Frank relaxing in the hot tub. Connor unlocked the door with his key card and stepped in. The smell of chlorine came sizzling through the air .

" Hey Connor ," Frank called from the hot tub .

" What's up dude ?" Connor called back.

Frank put back his head and closed his eyes " Just chilling ."
Connor set his belongings down on a nearby sun chair, and took off his shirt.

" The water's freezing ," Connor said , dipping his foot into the water .

" That's why I'm in the hot tub , that pool is as cold as a freaking lake ," Frank protested .

" It's not that bad !" Sarah exclaimed. " C'mon in Connor , it's not as bad as you think ."

" Ok ," Connor managed. He was very nervous. He was about to swim with the hottest girl in his league. Connor slowly walked into the pool and the water reached his chest.

 A couple of seconds later Frank stepped out of the hot tub, and made his way up the high dive platform . He climbed up the long narrow steps and made it to the top.

Connor , Jessica, and Sarah starred up in complete shock .

" Frank, what are you doing up there !" Jessica cried .

 Frank smiled in pride . " What does it look like I'm doing ? "

" You're out of your mind .Last summer you almost broke your neck," Sarah added in fear.

This wasn't going to end well.

Frank adjusted his goggles and bent his knees. Using all his momentum he leaped from the platform and came spurling down towards the water . He brought his knees into his chest and flipped 7 times in the air. He hit the shallow water in a perfect dive position.

" Holy guacamole ! "

" Is he dead ? "

" He's not coming up ."

After 1 minute of fear and panic Frank broke through the surface. His hair was damped and he was panting for breath.

" Hey guys !" Frank praised. " Are you happy to see me ? "

" Frank, you nearly scared us to death you idiot !"

Frank pulled back his hair and slipped out a long bellowing laugh .

" Why aren't you guys surprised ? I just did 7 flips of an extremely high platform and I don't get any applause ?"

Connor looked at Frank . "Dude, you should be in the Olympics ."

" Thanks ! I've been practicing a lot lately ," Frank said .

" I'm still surprised you didn't get hurt ! " Sarah chimed in .

The 4 shared a moment of laughter .

Frank swam around the pool for a little longer, then he decided to make his way back into the hot tub .

" Finally , the dofus is gone," Sarah said sarcastically .

" Yeah, I never thought he would leave ."

 Connor doggy paddled around the pool(which was embarrassing since he didn't know how to swim) and submerged his head underwater . He kicked his legs and began to swim down deeper. Each meter he went down, his ears began to pop. Connors lunges were screaming for air , and all he could see was darkness . He opened his eyes and was welcomed by the light and the everlasting shadows. How many minutes had he been under? Maybe 2 ? He couldn't tell. Connor never felt so cold and alone in his life. His heart was beating like a drum, each beat getting faster. A sudden urge of pain shot across Connor's chest . His lungs were beginning to swell as he made his way back up to the surface. Splash ! Connor shot out of the pool in a quick motion that startled Sarah and her friends by surprise . Connor was clearly not a good swimmer . Connor swam over to Sarah and splashed her in the face.

" Hey ," she squirmed, glancing over her shoulder. " Who did that ? "

" Catch me if you can," Connor taunted .

 " You're going to pay for this , Davidson … Big time !! "

The 2 began to splash each other , jokingly . Waves of water splashed against the pavement of the floor . Then before Connor expected it , Sarah released a huge title wave , as tall as the height of the ceiling . Before Connor could jump out of the way , the wave came crashing down and threw Connor 5 feet from the pool and onto the hard concrete . Connor came tumbling down , his hands shielding his face. Connor landed with a thud !He was sprawled on the ground all bruised up .

" Connor !! " Sarah screamed as she made her way out of the pool . She could see that Connor was clearly hurt and wasn't breathing.

"What have I done ? " Sarah thought to herself quietly .

" Connor, please answer me . Connor ?"

Still there was no response .

" What's going on out - OMG what happened !!" Frank shouted in surprise . He leaped out of the hot tub.

" Don't just stand there Frank ," Sarah called. " Do something ! "

Frank ran over to Connor and dropped down on his knees. He closed his eyes and his hands began to glow . Lightning crackled from his fingertips and up his veins. It was one of Frank's super abilities. Ever since Frank was struck by lightning at 5 year old, he had the power to control electricity .

" What were you trying to do ? " Frank asked. "Kill him ! "

" No, stupid," Sarah answered grudgently. " It was an accident ."

Frank put his hand on Connors' wrists and felt his pulse. He then put his ear to his heart, listening for any beating.

" He isn't breathing ."

" Please ," Sarah screamed. " Please Don't tell me he is dead."

" What's going on ? " Jessica said, stepping out of the pool. " Is everything ok ? "

 Jessica looked down and saw Connor lying motionless , blood running down the side of his head . Tears came sputtering down Jessica's face.

" How did this happen ?"

" You can blame it on your sis ," Frank barked , anger flashing before his eyes . " It was all her fault."

Jessica turned towards Sarah . " How could you do such a thing ?"

" It was an accident ,ok? I swear I didn't mean it . We were having fun and all of a sudden the next thing I know , I see Connor laying on the ground. Whatever happened wasn't me . I - I couldn't control it ."

" I thought Dr. Hill was teaching us this ," Jessica glanced at Sarah and Frank ." You know how to control your powers ."

"Well , I guess I couldn't ," Sarah stormed. " Goss , why are you blaming everything on me? We all will be in the same amount of trouble if Mr . Anderson finds out about this ."

" What should we do ? " said Frank

Sarah looked down at Frank . " Frank, I want you to keep trying, do whatever you have to do to bring him back ."

" Well you see it's not that simple ."

" What do you mean ? "

Frank became serious . " I mean I can't use my powers near water ... if you paid attention in science class you would know that if electricity gets near water , it causes high voltage which can easily kill you ."

" But if you do it you may be able to save Connor's life ."

" If I did it , it would mean I would have to die . And heck I don't want to die today."

" Then do you have any more brilliant ideas ? "

" Hmm- ," Frank thought. " Maybe we should try CPR ."

" I'm not doing it ," Sarah protested. " I'm not kissing his lips. That's gross ."

" Fine, Then I'll do it," Frank said savagely. Frank closed his eyes and the electricity from his hands disappeared. Frank scooted closer to Connor . Frank had to think back on his training in medical class. Everything he learned came down to this moment. It depended on the life of his best friend. Frank put his mouth against Connors and began to do huge rescue breaths. He did this a few times while pinching Connors nose.

"C'mon buddy ," Frank whispered. "Wake up " . Connor remained still on the ground . His lips were blue and blood oozed from his head. Frank kept repeating the routine , trying to hold back the tears that were too eager to let go.

" Please Connor ," Frank repeated. "Don't die on me ."

Sarah and Jessica remained silent , Watching in disbelief.

" I think he's breathing ," Frank called . " I can feel his pulse ."

Connor opened his eyes , and bolted straight up. He began coughing water out of his mouth.

" Connor ! " The 2 girls ran over to him gripping him in a bear-like hug.

" I'm so sorry ," Sarah exclaimed . Connor stared around the room, touching the back of his head .

" Go grab a towel, " Frank ordered. Jessica obeyed.

" Here you go ," Jessica threw the towel towards Frank.

Frank cradled Connor in his arms and put the towel around the back of his head .

" This should hopefully stop the bleeding ."

Connors' focus was blurred and he was confused. " What's going on, " he managed .

" It's Ok ," Sarah rested her hand on Connor . " Everything is going to be alright."

Frank looked worryingly into Sarah's eyes . " Do you think he has a concussion? should we take him to the hospital wing ?"

Sarah nodded quietly.

" Let's go every one one ," Frank said to the group, " I think we've had enough fun for today ."

Chapter 8 : poisoned product

Adam Magee put on his finest suit . He adjusted his bowtie , slicked back his hair , and made his way out of his small residential cottage . The cool air pushed back against his face , and the sound of birds echoed across a nearby forest . It was a little past 7: 00 am in the small town of Virginia . Farmers and workers were up and about with their business , and cars were zooming across the highways . Adam needed to get out of the house. He had been cooped up for months , so he decided to treat himself to a nice morning breakfast . Before he left he double checked his pockets. He made sure he had a face mask and a bottle of hand sanitizer , as well as a few loads of cash . A global pandemic was still going on , and the least thing Adam wanted was to get sick .   The young man continued his way on a gravel path, leading him across streets of fancy restaurants and candy shops . He could smell the brewing of fresh milk chocolate , and the odor of gumdrops. No one was hardly in town on this particular day . There were a few workers behind the counters, and an old lady in a coffee shop but other than that the town remained quiet . The global virus really had destroyed the economy . No one was hardly out anymore, and the world felt so lonely and empty . It was the first time Adam had been back in town for quite a while . He was so used to watching television and reading magazines that he wasn't used to the outside world . He took a deep breath and carried on with his journey , knowing he had to move on with his life . Adam crossed the street , and quickly passed a homeless man sitting on a bench . He looked really skinny and out of shape. He had baggy large pants that went down to his ankles, and a dity gray jacket full of holes . Adam could tell he was desperate for money . But what was he to care for, he had his own money and life to deal with ! A little after 7:30 a large billboard could be seen across the street .

Eddies Diner : open 7:30 to 12:00 pm

Perfect ! He had just arrived on time .   Adam hurried up the steps of the old fashioned restaurant , his shoes taping rapidly against the concrete . He opened the glass door and peered into the diner . It looked old fashioned and out of date. A juicebox played in the corner .   The music was Elvis Presley . The floor was black and white and the booths were decorated red. There was 1 worker working on the job , and 2 chefs in the back . **Clearly business was not going well** . The sound of a ringing bell echoed across the restaurant, startling the group of workers .

" Well hello there ," the waitress said politely . " How may i help you today."

" Table for 1 please ."

The old woman grabbed a stack of menus from underneath the counter and looked across the room .

" I can seat you in a booth in the back if that's ok ?"

" Sure , anything will work ," he affirmed .

The old lady nodded her head .

" Ok, right this way…. you can follow me towards the back ."

The 2 of them made their way towards a medium sized table filled with napkins and silverware . Across the table a group of teenagers were enjoying a stack of pancakes .

" Is there anything I can get you to drink ? we got orange juice, apple juice, and black roast coffee ."

Adam scanned across the menu .

" I think I'll have a cup of double espresso coffee… and can you add 2 creams and 2 sugars ?"

"You got it, honey ," the waitress called , scribbling down on her notepad. "I will come back for your order in just a few minutes ."

Adam took off his coat . He set down his scarf and ruled up his sleeves .

A little more than 2 minute passed and the waitress had returned . She was holding a tray with a bottle of cold water and a double espresso coffee held in a white tea cup.

" Here you go ," the waitress placed the cups on the table." Do you need more time or are you ready to order ? "

Adam skimmed one last time at the menu . He had made his decision .

" No , I think I'm set to order ."

" Ok . What can I get for you ? "

" I'll take a short stack of chocolate chip pancakes, an order of eggs, and a side of bacon and sausage ."

" How would you like your egg cooked ? " the waitress asked .

" Scrambled ."

" And would you like some whip cream and strawberries on your shortstack as well ? "

" Yes please ."

The waitress jotted down the order on her notepad .

" Alright then, the food should be out soon ."

The waitress grabbed the menus off the table , making her way to the kitchen .

....

After Adam finished his meal , he signed the bill and left a 20 dollar tip , since he was feeling generous. He slipped on his coat and walked out of the diner , the chime of the bell ringing behind. Adam made his way home , quickly and about . After crossing Taylor Street Adam felt dizzy, and nauseous. His head hurt and his stomach felt empty. Maybe he had caught a flu bug, or maybe there was something in the food. Adam became unstable, he felt like the whole world was a merry go around. Adam vomited on the pavement, steading himself on a lamp poll. He felt so weak and tired he just wanted to lie down. Adam fell to his knees , white saliva spilling out of his mouth. His head hit the concrete and all he remembered was darkness.

Chapter 9: Day 1

Connor awoke to a bright sunny day . The sun was set behind the clouds , and the morning birds sang their happy songs . It was around 8:30 when Connor awoke from his bed . He glanced at the clock startled by how late it was . He had overslept !! nervous and full of panic, Connor quickly changed into a pair of sweatpants and a white t-shirt , and made his way towards the dining hall. He snatched a banana and a granola bar to go , as well as a mango smoothie.   Connor would need the energy and protein for the long day ahead !   30 minutes later, Connor proceeded through the long narrow hallways on the 14th floor . He then came across room 305. When he entered he saw a group of students sitting formally on desks , jotting down on pen and paper.

" If it isn't Connor Davidson ! " Mr .Hill said , a tall skinny man with huge spectacles . " Mister, you do know you're 30 minutes late right ?"

Connor stood in the doorway embarrassed of himself . He knew he had made a horrible first impression .

"Yes sir .. I'm really sorry I couldn't make it on time . I overslept and I -."

Mr. Hill cut off Connor before he could speak another word.

" Listen ... In my class you follow my rules and my expectations . That includes getting to class on time " , he said sternly ." Do I make myself clear ? " Mr. Hill clarified .

Connor gulped .

" Yes sir ."

"Good ."

Mr. Hill led Connor to a desk in the far corner.

" This will be your new seat ... please sit down and take out your blue spiral notebook . We are going to take some notes , so I expect you to stay focused and pay attention ," Mr. Hill explained as he now made his way back to the front of the room .

Connor nodded his head, and made his way towards his seat . He took out a large notebook from the inside of the desk , and pulled out a sharpened pencil .

Mr. Hill cleared his throat and stared at the class.

" Ok everyone, Today we will be learning about our superhero abilities and methods you can use to control them . We will also be covering the topic of how to use our powers in a dangerous situation ."

The whole class moaned.

" C'mon people ," Mr. Hill shrieked. " We have a test on this tomorrow which is worth 100 percent of your grade. I want all of you to do well."

Mr. Hill turned his back towards the class and began to write on the board

 " Rule number 1 , never use your powers against others . I can't tell you how important this rule is ! Every year someone is severely injured or hurt due to the mistreatment of power . I want all of you to only express your superhero abilities during a mission, or when you're told to. But that is it ," Mr. Hill looked around the class making sure everyone was still listening . " If you are caught bullying someone, or hurting someone with your superpowers inside or outside of the school's boundaries , then you will be in serious trouble . So can you all promise me to use your powers wisely ?"

Connor and the rest of the class nodded their heads .

" Very well , we can now move onto rule number 2 ! Now rule number 2 is by far the most important . If you feel like you're not able to control your powers in any circumstance , then it is best you follow these simple instructions ." Mr. Hill pulled out a new piece of chalk and wrote the following on the chalkboard .

#1 = take deep breaths
  #2 = self talk
  #3 = step away from the situation
   " All of these steps will prevent the situation from escalating and will keep you younglings safe from being endangered ."

Connor raised his hand .

"Mr. Hill, I have a question ."

Mr. Hill spun towards Connor . " Go on ."

" Well, I was just wondering, what happens if these steps don't work . What if your powers are just so powerful that you can't control them ?"

Mr. Hill gave this serious thought . " Mr . Davidson ," he said in a chilling tone . " Are you suggesting that you were under the circumstance of this happening ? "

" No sir ," Connor lied.

" I sure hope so . " Mr. Hill stared at Connor seriously. " If a human being was incapable of empowering themselves , then they could be highly dangerous . Causing tyranny and destruction to this world . Millions of innocent lives would be taken , and the person held responsible would destroy the earth as we know it ."

  " I understand, sir ."

" Good , because I don't want to hear you bring it up again ."

....

After a long busy day of lessons, Connor was feeling tired. He took 3 other classes that day , including combat training , medical class , as well as a lesson on superpower techniques . In all Connors classes he did very poorly. He couldn't jump a inch from the ground without landing on his face, or even do a simple task that was instructed . Connors' hopes were beginning to die down . He realized that maybe he was a zero , not a hero. The only class Connor really liked[and was good at] was combat training. He loved fighting with swords and learning all the strikes and blows .The other classes were plain old boring . In Connor's lesson on super power techniques, he managed to make a ball of flame the size of a beach ball. Everyone thought it was cool until one of the students caught on fire. Long story short.   By the end of the day Connor was worn out . He felt like spending the rest of the evening in the library , or going to the bowling alley on the 10th floor . Of course Connor had quite a lot of homework . By the time he left his final class of the day he was holding 20 stacks of lab sheets . He had never received so much homework in his life ! A little after 4:00 pm Connor was back in his dorm room . He was sitting on the couch studying for an exam , while eating a bag of pretzels . Of course Connor was completely stumped and hardly knew anything about super abilities , but he did try his best to make the best out of it . Connor didn't know how long it would take to complete all this work , but he knew he would most likely be occupied for the rest of the night .

There was a knock on the door . " Hello, can I come in ? " the voice called.

Connor bolted up from his chair .

" Just a second ." Connor was startled by surprise. It was almost 10:00 pm and someone was knocking on his door ? Without hesitation Connor opened it . He was greeted by a young lady with curly taffe hair and blue eyes. She was wearing a pink skirt with Nike trainers. She looked very pretty.

" Hi ... Sarah ," Connor greeted, blushing a little bit .

Sarah smiled .

" Are you going to let me in or just stand there ?"

" Oh... right ," Connor said awkwardly . " Sorry ." Connor closed the door behind him.

" What is it ? "

" I wanted to talk to you ," Sarah proclaimed .

" Well I have quite a lot of homework to catch up on, but I guess I can take a short break, " Connor said .

Sarah took a seat on Connors bed. " How's your head ? " she said worryingly.

Connor put his hand on his bandaged scalp .

" Well you know it's getting better . I went to the nurse yesterday and she said it's nothing serious ."

" Well that's good. Like i said i'm really sorry about yest-."

Connor cut her off .

" Don't worry about it , it was an accident ."

Sarah smiled . " On a scale of 1 to 10 how much does it hurt ? "

Connor gave this thought . " Well if you really want to know I feel like a 2 ."

Sarah kissed the top of Connor's head . Connors heart was tangled in butterflies . " That's good to hear."

There was an awkward moment of silence .

" So how was your first day of lessons ?" Sarah asked, trying to break the silence .

Connor shrugged his shoulders .

" Well it was pretty good , except for the intention of being a complete failure ."

Sarah was caught off guard . " So it really was that bad huh ? "

" Yeah , you could say that . I can't do anything right , all the other kids can shoot lasers out of their eyes   and dodge bullets, and all I can do is shoot stupid fireballs out of my hands and set a classroom on fire ! "

 " Don't think of an ability as a mistake, think of it as a talent . Do you know how lucky you are? I bet every kid wants to be special like you ."

Connor rolled his eyes . " What's cool about having fire powers ? All you can do is cook hamburgers and cause more trouble for the fire department. "

" I'm telling you , by the end of the year you will be able to do amazing things ... just give yourself time , you've only been here for 1 day Connor !"

" I guess you're right ," Connor babbeld . " I guess I should give myself more time ."

Sarah glanced at Connor carefully . There were large bags under his eyes, and he seemed not like his usual self .

" Are you alright, Connor ? you like really tired ," she asked .

" Yeah I'm fine, it's just been a really long day for me and I have a ton of homework to do ."

Sarah nodded her head .

" I get it ."

" Yeah, Mr. Hill said we have a test tomorrow and he wants the whole class to do well ."

" Well if you'd like I can help you study ."

Connor locked his eyes in Sarahs . " You really mean it ? "

" Of course ..... I love helping people ," she said calmly .

....

After 11:30 pm Sarah was packing up her things . She gave Connor a hug, and made her way out the door . Connor thought that Sarah was a really good instructor . She helped him memorize all of the categories of power, and made learning really fun . When Connor was stumped with a question Sarah would break down the steps one by one until Connor fully understood it . Connor wished Sarah could have stayed a little longer, but by the time they were finished it was already past their bedtimes . Connors first day at the Heroes Academy was off to a troubling start. He had failed many times, and was hardly good at anything . But as Connor slipped into bed that night he wondered what tomorrow would bring him .

Chapter 10 : gone missing

Mister and Misses Davidson were starting to worry. Their only son, Connor, had been missing for the last 2 days and they had no idea where he could have gone. Later that night the two went to the local police station. They filed a report on a missing child and were asked lots of questions .

" Mr. Davidson ," Cherief Hopkins said ." Do you have any idea where your son could have gone ? "

" No officer ," Mr . Davidson said worryingly ." We don't have a clue ."

The general took a munch on his glazed donut. " Then there's nothing we can riley do ma'am ," he looked at the 2 occupants." I am Really sorry."

" Are son is missing ! " Mrs. Davison screamed. " And you're going to do nothing about it ? "

" Stay calm ," officer Hopkins demanded. " You don't have to shout."

 Mrs. Davidson rose up from her chair . " How can I stay calm? Our little boy is missing and who knows if he's even alive . So don't tell me to relax ."

" We are trying our best , ma'am. I've sent officers on duty to look around and keep a lookout ," The general explained . " We've put up signs all across the neighborhood ."

Mrs. Davidson sat back in her chair.

" They're doing everything they can, " Mr. Davidson assured his wife. " They will find Connor and bring him home. "

Mrs. Davison took a deep breath.

" I'm just scared . That's all ."

" I am too ," Mr. Davison said . " But we have the hope for the best and think positive ", the two held each other's hands.

" Can you give me a description of what he looks like?" The general commanded .

Mrs. Davidosn took a shaky breath. " He's about 5ft with blonde hair and green eyes."

Officer Hopkins scribbled down on his notepad . " When did you last see him?"

" 2 nights ago ," Mr. Davidson answered. "Me and my wife were out having lunch and when we came home he wasn't there."

The deputy slicked his mustache . " Was there anything that could have provoked your son from possibly running away ? "

" Well , we did ground him for a week and Connor has been very depressed lately . "

" Iam no psychiatrist , Mrs. and Mr. Davidson ," officer Hopkins proclaimed. "But... I do know that when a child experiences a rough situation, it can aggravate them to feel like they don't belong, which causes them to syscalasgically want to run away . So my theory is that maybe Connor felt this way ."

" What have we done?" Mr. Davidson squealed , putting his head in his hands. "We've failed in our parenting ."

"Please Connor ," Mrs. Davidson whispered to herself. " Please come home."

Chapter 11: breaking news !

Sydney Rodriguez stood in front of a television screen , a microphone in her hand and a story that would change the world . 500 million people were sitting in their homes waiting for the report , Jonathan Mcdwell was just one of the few . Jonathan was at his large luxury home sitting in his bathtub with a cigarette attracted to his mouth .Candles were displayed along the sides of the tub including a bottle of champagne . The sound of the wind could be heard from the screen, and the young reporter made her appearance . Today she wore a yellow raincoat, and red sparkly boots. Her hair was tied in a bun and a golden necklace was hanging down her chest , as well as a mask that could be seen covering her mouth and nose. She took a long deep breath and started her report .

" Good morning Americans, my name is Sydney Rodriguez and today I am here at Eddie's Diner just across the 57th street in Virginia . " A small old fashioned restaurant could be seen in the background .

" This morning a man named Adam Magee was seen entering the diner at around 7:30 am . He came in for his usual breakfast and coffee, but something did not go as expected ." The reporter changed her expression.

" However, when Adam left the diner he collapsed to the ground . investigators reported that they found his body in a nearby street where they claimed he was severely sick ." A disturbing image of a elderly man covered in vomit could be seen on the screen .

Thousands of viewers were startled by the details . How could such a thing happen ?

" Now this isn't the first time we've seen something like this, folks. In the past week millions of people have been getting poisoned from the foods served at local restaurants all across America . Food products have been spreading sickness and disease , including a new variant of the global virus ."

A sickening smile came across the mad man's face . Indeed his plan was working after all! He and his crew of elite scientists had been working for weeks on a new antidote that would kill more people, and it seemed like his dreams were coming true . . Jonathan had decided the only way to continue the spread of the virus was to put toxins and dangerous chemicals in food products , which would definitely be a more efficient way to spread his global disease . If Jonathan's company could continue to provide more samples of this antipodate, and continue poisoning foods across the world, then before long Jonathan would have the chance to take over the world .

"We recommend everyone for the time being stays in lock down, while being extra cautious when buying food . We don't want anyone else to get sick, or have a higher chance of spreading the virus ," Sydney Rodriguez continued .

"We for sure don't know who is behind this terrible crisis, but police officials are on the case .... but in the meantime stay safe everyone and I'll see you tomorrow on channel 9 ."

The TV channel blackened and the report came to an end. Viewers were traumatized by everything that they had just heard, and could hardly move from their seats . This virus was getting worse by the day , and it wouldn't be long until humanity would be wiped out . The world only wondered when all of this would come to an end.

Chapter 12 : the test

Mr. Hill paced around in his classroom as he watched the rhythm of a ticking clock. He glanced at his first year students proudly, a stack of papers gripped tightly in his hands . Students were gathered in their seats with nervous looks on their faces . Today was their first exam , and no one wanted to fail [especially in Mr. hill's class] . The teacher walked down the rows of desks and began to pass out long packets of paper. Tons of questions could be seen scattered all across the sheets , including a corner where you would have to write your class period. Connor was at the back of the class with sweat dripping down his face . He knew he was prepared for this exam, but anxiety was taking over . He tapped his foot rapidly on the ground waiting to take the test . The other students in the class were trembling with fear . Their hands were shaking as they received their packets .

" Do not begin your test yet ..... Please wait until I give you further instructions ," Mr. Hill said loudly .

The students were beginning to already flip through their exams as they read the questions carefully . Connor had still not received his yet, but he was nervous when he saw Mr. Hill coming his way .

" And here you go," he said gently .

Connor accepted it .

" Thank you ."

Mr. Hill made his way back towards the front of the room and put his hands together .

" Now as you all know you are about to take your first exam of trimester 1 !

No cheating will be prohibited as well as copying off other students. Do I make myself clear ?"

" Yes," the group shouted.

 "Now if I see any of you breaking these instructions, then I'm afraid your test will not be scored, and you will be sent to Dr. Sanchez's office immediately . "

The students paid close attention .

" You will have 75 minutes to complete this exam, if you don't finish in the given time then you may report back here during free period .. There are 10 pages provided . You must explain all of your thoughts and reasoning in detail , and try to answer the questions as thoroughly as you can. "

The class remained silent .

" Any questions ?" Mr. Hill asked as he glanced across the room .

No hands went up .

" Ok , then you are now excused to begin the test !"

Connor quickly wrote his name on top of his sheet of paper and glanced at the first set of questions .

#1 = how can you control your superpowers in a given circumstance ?

> **A = take deep breaths**
> **b= self talk**
> **C = step away from the situation**
> **D = all of the above**

Connor of course knew the answer ! it was definitely D , he remembered from last class that all of these steps should be used when you're not able to control your abilities ! He hovered his pencil over the final option and circled it .

The first question was done, [which in fact was a piece of cake] but he knew the other questions were definitely not going to be this easy .

#2 = what is rule number #1 , and explain its cause and effect in detail !

 A small blank space was provided below the question . Connor reread the question for the 2nd time, and jotted down what had come to mind .

= Rule #1 states " never use your powers against others " . This rule is very important to follow because if you don't use your powers wisely you could severely hurt someone, or cause greater danger ! if you were to use your powers against someone then you would highly be expelled from Heroes Academy , causing you to lose your hero privileges .

Connor wrapped up his final sentence and scratched his head . He read his paragraph one last time making sure he had provided all the details , and then moved onto the next question .

#3 = in which situation should you use your powers ? Please circle 2 possible answers .

A = to bully or threaten someone

b= in class

3= when someone is in danger

4= while fighting

Another easy question , the 2 possible answers were 3 , and 4 ! of course option A did not make sense because it went against rule #1 , and B i guess could make sense but Mr. Hill never mentioned anything about it. So without hesitation Connor circled the last 2 possible answers . Connor continued to fill out answers until time was up . The test wasn't as bad as he thought, most of the things he studied didn't show up, and the questions were pretty much straightforward . By the time the 75 minutes were up Connor was already finished . His sheet was covered with answers and lots of explanations . Connor knew he had done really well on the test , and his stress died down .

" Alright everyone pencils down, our 75 minutes are up ."

A few kids in the front of the class were still on page 3 of the test ,and hardly had gotten anything done . Connor knew they were pretty wasting their time and goofing off . Mr. Hill went around the classroom as he collected everyone's sheets . The students in the classroom began to stretch their arms and legs, including Connor himself . He had been sitting in a chair for nearly an hour and a half and his body was completely stiff . The teacher grabbed the final test and set them down carefully on his table . He took out his watch and glanced at it carefully . Class would end in about 5 minutes .

" Alright everyone we have 5 minutes left of class, I don't have anything else for you today so you can spend the rest of your time doing whatever you'd like ... but please don't make too much noise, there's still classes going on and I'd hate to disrupt them ."

The volume began to pick up , and kids began talking to one another . Left with nothing to do , Connor pulled out a copy of Harry Potter from his backpack and spent the rest of the class reading .

Chapter 13 : franks story [9 years ago]

Dont be out too long was the last words Frank heard before the accident . He was a chubby little 5 year old at the time who often spent his weekends at the ice cream shop and candy store in town . His parents always forced him to go outside because he would never leave the house . He would sit in his room for hours still in his pajamas until the start of a new day . His parents had tried to get him into sports and physical activities when he was younger but nothing seemed to work . He would cry and shout , and make a whole scene wherever he went . So by the time he turned 7 his parents were tired of putting up with him . On a clear foggy day in April , a shower of rain and thunder struck the small village of Chicago . Trees were dancing like crazy , and the wind was howling like a beast . Sightings of lighting were seen all across the city, and cars were stuck in traffic . Believe it or not, Frank liked the rain . It was the only thing he liked other than his obsession with food . So when he woke up to drops of rain pouring down his window shill , he quickly put on his yellow raincoat and ran outside . His mother was in the kitchen making a batch of scrambled eggs, when all of a sudden she was startled by his son's awakening .

"Woah , woah, woah , where do you think you're going ?" she exclaimed .

Frank turned around from the doorway and looked at his mother .

"Mama, do you see? It's running outside ! I want to go play ."

Frank's mother put her hand on her hip.

"I don't think you should go out there sweetie pie . The forecast is really bad and it's not safe . Why don't you come sit at the table and eat your breakfast ." She pointed to a tall plate of french toast and sausage .

" I'm also cooking some scrambled eggs. Your favorite ."

Frank opened the door, not interested in the food .

" Not now mama, I really want to go outside ! "

Frank's mother was starstruck . She didn't know what to say .

"Fine, but don't be out for too long , I don't want you getting hurt ," she said sternly .

Frank began to jump up in joy . He ran over to his mother and gave her a tight squeeze .

"Yay!! Thank you mama ."

Before Frank's mother could say another word her son was already out the door .

....

Frank jumped around in a pile of puddles , as a spark of thunder came crashing to the ground . KABAM !!! A spark of fire lit up against the courtyard in a flash . Frank was startled by the strike and backed up against a nearby wall . The fire died down and diseapred to its normal form . Frank leaned away from the wall and looked at the sky above him . It was still really foggy and rain was coming down hard .No more lightning had been seen so Frank leaped to another puddle . Splash ! Splash ! His shoes went as he jumped happily on the still water . He didn't know how long he had been out here for , but all ke knew was that he had stayed longer than expected .

"Frank , it's time to come home !" a loud voice rattled across the courtyard.

 He knew the voice, it was his mother . Frank sighed deeply, He wasn't ready to come home just yet .

"Frank ! Frank ! Your breakfast is getting cold ," Franks mother protested

.

" Can I have 5 more minutes ?" Frank asked pleadingly .

Mrs. Roberts crossed her arms and stepped out onto the doorstep .

" No ! you promised me you would come in when i asked ."

Frank was full of anger . He hated when his mother didn't let him do what he wanted .

" Why can't I do the things I want to do ? You always boss me around and tell me what to do . I'm not going home , I want to stay out here ," Frank protested .

Mrs. Roberts grabbed her son by his collar and pushed him back inside the house . Frank screamed and yelled like a cry baby . His mother always hated when he acted like this !

" Stop it right now !"

" No ! No ! No ! Let me go ."

Mrs. Robert yanked him harder than expected , accidently sending her son splashing to the ground . Frank fell into a gigantic puddle of rain and mud, his body was a complete mess . Boiling anger filled into Frank's head , he was so mad at her all he wanted to do was run away .Without hesitation the 5 year old ran across the street away from his home hoping to find somewhere else to play .
" Come back here frank this instant ! I'm going to have a long talk with you when you come home ." Frank didn't seem to hear his mother, he was running so fast that his mother would never catch him . He took a small break across the street , taking heavy deep breaths of air . up ahead another strike of lighting made its appearance . It struck a nearby home causing it to explode in a rage of flames . Then another strike started, then another , then another , and another . More flames of hot heat shifted across the entire streets , causing cars to back up and make their escape . Frank was startled by everything he had just seen . He no longer wanted to spend the rest of the day outside, it was way too dangerous ! If a spark of lighting struck Frank he knew he would be dead meat .He put the yellow hood back on his head , and ran back the way he came from. He never ran so fast in his life !

....

Being struck by lighting is one of the worst pains you could ever have !
[well that's at least what frank thought .] By the time he had made it back
home the storm was becoming more powerful . Channel signals were
going out like crazy, and more lighting had been spotted. Frank entered
the famimilar courtyard , continuing his fast run . He was just 10 meters
away when he felt the lighting strike him . It was a jolting excruciating pain
that flowed throughout his body . His ears began to ring ,and his vision
began to fade. Frank collapsed to the ground in agony . He tried to move
but the pain kept him motionless .

" Frank ! What happened ? "

Frank slowly lifted his head up from the pavement and glared at his
mother . He was too defeated to let out a word .

" Mommy......I...... Hurt ....," was all the little boy could say .

Mrs. Roberts put her hands over her mouth as she watched her defeated
son . She was never so scared in her life . She got on her knees and
prayed, hoping everything was going to be alright .

....

Being a superhero is cool . Ever since I got struck by lightning I've never
felt happier in my life. I can shoot lightning bolts out of my hands , and
control electricity ! How cool is that ? Now I'm not trying to brag or
anything , but I think I might just have the coolest superpower in the
universe . For the past 2 weeks I've been testing out my powers . I like to
show my friends at school everything I can do, and sometimes I like to
show off for Becky Anderson [A.K.A my crush] . But it wasn't until later
that summer when I received the letter that would change my life . I woke
up to the sound of the doorbell on a bright sunny day in July . I quickly
got on a t-shirt and went to the front door . I looked around for a second
not seeing anything but a man walking his dog, and a paperboy
delivering the morning paper . But then I caught something out of the
corner of my eye . On the front step a large red envelope could be seen . It
had a big yellow ribbon and beautiful stars skidded to the left and right .
Curious to know what it was , I brought the letter inside . I set it down on
the kitchen table and took a seat on a nearby stool. The first thing I
noticed about the letter was that it had my name on it ! I hardly ever
received mail . An address was labeled on the bottom right corner, as well

as a superhero logo dented right in the middle : **Heroes Academy : home of the heroes** the label read . A smile came to my face . The fun was about to begin ....

Chapter 14 : sarah's story [7 years ago]

Sarah was sea sick . It wasn't the first time she was on a cruise , in fact she was always traveling. Her parents were journalists who worked for a newspress , and had a lot of money ! Sarah lived in a rich neighborhood and often could get whatever she wanted. The truth was that She was spoiled . Very spoiled. For Christmas that year she got a new Iphone , EarPods, and even a Gucci bag. Lucky !

" I think I'm going to throw up ," Sarah trembled . " Can we get off the boat?"

" Sit down ," her father answered ." You need to sit down and relax. "

Sarah's face turned pale as molded cheese. " My stomach hurts, " she wailed. " I feel dizzy ."

Mr. Robinson laid Sarah on a nearby bed ."Lay down sweatie , and rest." He handed her a banana. "And eat this. It will help with stopping the nausea."

Sarah accepted it weakly . " Thank you ." She took a bite of her banana .

" The bathrooms right next door ," Her father pointed across the hall. " If you need it ."

" Ok ," Sarah managed. " I think I'll go do that ." Sarah got up from her bed and walked across the hallway, as the boat rocked back and forth. She felt mis balanced and uneasy. Sarah opened the bathroom door and locked it behind her. She then did her thing and washed her hands with soap and water. She then stared into the mirror. She saw her reflection staring back at her. Sarah thought for a moment , in peace. She hated this trip already and wished she and her family had never come in the first place. She had to agree that California was pretty cool with the tall palm trees and Hollywood boulevard , but other than that there was nothing that interesting. The thing she hated the most was being on the cruise ship. She hated having to share a bunk with her younger brother and eating the all you can Eat buffets (especially because they served raw fish) . She was sick of the sightseeing and the family photos that her parents made her pose for . Long story short, it takes like quizzillion   tries for the perfect family photo.   But if there was one thing Sarah hoped for more than anything , it was that she wanted to go home. If only it was that easy. She and her family were not leaving till Saturday , which gave her a whole nother week to spare. Some kids considered Sarah lucky to be on a vacation in San Francisco , more or less be on a private class cruise. Sarah felt no sympathy whatsoever on what anybody else thought, she just cared about herself.

" Are you alright in there? " a voice called out .

" Be right out ," Sarah called back . She pushed back a strand of hair and unlocked the top lock of the door.

" What took you so long ? " Sara's father questioned. " It's been almost 10 minutes ."

 " Sorry ," Sarah blushed ." My stomach has been hurting ."

" I understand sweetie ," her father said in a reassuring tone. " Anyway, I think it's time for breakfast ," Mr . Robinson glanced at his watch. " It's already ten clock ."

Sarah nodded .

....

Sarah and her father made their way to the dinning hall. It had crystal chandeliers hanging from the ceiling and tall oak chairs. There was a huge buffet table topped with Belgian waffles, Bacon , omelts , fresh fruit , and yogurt. Sarah had to admit , it looked riley delicious. Sarah grabbed a plate and loaded on everything she could get. She still wasn't that hungry but she needed to eat something. Her father insisted. Sarah grabbed some forks and utensils and made her way to a nearby table. Her father joined her .

" How's your omelet ? " he asked.

Sarah put her fork down. " It's very good ."

Her father smiled . " I am glad to hear that ."

The 2 ate the rest of their meal in silence . Sarah munched on her yogurt and her fruit cup, while her father read the morning paper with a glass of freshly squeezed orange juice . After breakfast the 2 stepped outside onto the boat's balcony . Sarah squinted her eyes and looked into the horizon . It was beautiful ! She could see the crystal blue skies and the warming evening sun reflecting across the water.

" Isn't it beautiful ? " Sarah's father remarked.

Sarah nodded . " It's wonderful ."

The cruise ship sailed across the waters , making its journey north. It was only 3 hours until it landed in the bahamas. On the boat there were swimming pools , restaurants , as well as bowling alleys. The cost was unbelievable. Only people with money could afford it .

" I am going to go get a drink, do you want anything ? "

" I'm ok ," Sarah said .

" I insist ," her father commented. " I'll get you a kiddie cocktail ."

When her father came back , Sarah accepted her glass . Her and her father sat on nearby sun chairs and put their heads back.

" Are you excited about going to the Bahamas ? " her father questioned.

Sarah took a bite of a cherry. " I guess ," she replied in an unconvincing voice.

Her father looked at her. " I know you hate this trip , honey . I know you'd rather be at home ."

Sarah gulped . " Dad , I love it here , " she lied. " Why would you think that?"

Sarah's father took a sip of his whisky. " You just seem not like herself. "

Sarah couldn't lie any further. Though she wanted to make her father proud , she couldn't get it past him.

" I'm sorry ," Sarah proclaimed . " It's just that, I am not happy."

Her father looked concerned. " You can talk to me , you know I'm always here for you . "

Sarah took a deep breath. " Some families dream of being rich. They want million dollar homes , fancy sports cars and they want to live a perfect lifestyle . But what about the outsiders, the bumbs , what about the people who have to sleep in their cars. Shouldn't we be helping them? If there was one thing I learned it's that money can't buy you happiness. I Am not happy daddy, and it's because I don't live a decent life. Everywhere I go there's cameras flashing or herds of mobs attacking me. I want to be normal for once, daddy, is that too hard to ask ?"

Mr. Robinson held her daughter's hand. " I'm so sorry Sarah," He cried." I'm sorry I didn't understand what you were going through. "

Sarah let out a tear." It's ok . If there's one thing I am happy about more than anything it's being with you."

The 2 shared a warm smile .

" I love you Sarah ."

" I love you dad." The two embraced.

Suddenly out of the blue , a siren wailed through the boat. Lights began to flash and a voice came through the intercom.

" This is Captain Fritz," the voice called ." I need everybody to evacuate the ship immediately."

The passengers panicked .

" Our boat has unexpectedly crashed and we need everyone aboard to evacuate , I repeat ."

" You will find life preservers under the seats . I want everyone to put it on and try to swim across the shore."

"We need to do this quickly and fast ," the voice finished .

" What's going on dad ? What's happening to the ship ?" Sarah asked in a stage of panic . All around her thousands of passengers were running around like crazy . There was a lot of screaming which made Sarah even more frightened .

" Honey everything is going to be ok ? Just listen to my instructions and we'll get out of here safely ."

" How about Matthew ? "

" Your brother will be ok. He will make it out. I promise."

Sarah was on the urge of tears." I don't want to die daddy."

Mr. Rodrigez took a deep breath and grabbed his daughter's hand . Sarah and her father leaped up from their chairs and put on their life jackets. They then dived into the water head first. Sarah screamed in the air, as they came landing down. Sarah's head was submerged under water, and all she could see was darkness and bubbles. The water was freezing cold causing Sarah to begin to shiver. Sarah broke through the surface, and to her surprise the floaties kept her and her father afloat.

" We have to swim, " Sarah's father called. "Can you do it ?"

Sarah nodded. When he looked behind her he could see the other passengers screaming and jumping off the boat's platform. She tried to look away. She saw her younger brother in the distance . She was glad he was okay. Sarah and her father kicked their legs and arms and began to swim to shore. Even though Sarah had her life jacket on, she was beginning to get tired. Then when Sarah and her father least expected it , a huge titield wave as tall as a skyscraper came crashing down. Sarah and her father were thrown down deep into the abyss , pitch darkness over taking them.

My name is Sarah Robbinson and you heard my story. You may be wondering , what happened after the boat wreck incident? Well my friends, if there's one thing you probably guessed it's that I am alive. The only sad news was that my father didn't make it . Ohh and there's one thing I forgot to mention, it's that I have super powers. Which I didn't discover until that day . I knew how to walk on water (you can call me Jesus) and control tidal waves. You can also call me the Daughter of Poseidon if you want but I'd rather have you call me Water girl. I know , I know many people are going to hate that name but that's all I could come up with . After I blacked out, I woke up in this underwater palace. There I was raised by dolphins and mermaids . I learned how to control my water abilities and some specatlarly things. Right now I'm at the Hero's academy and enjoying the rest of my teenage life. Fun fact about me , I am a book nerd and my favorite series is Harry potter. But If there's one thing I still haven't accomplished it's to tell Connor I love him . Maybe I'll have the guts to tell him one day , maybe....

Chapter 15: martial arts

"Mr. Davidson ," Sensei Aia called ." Can you please step up on the mat?"

Connor looked around the room ." Me ?" he asked curiously .

" Yes .We need a volunteer and you're going to demonstrate for us,"he finished .

It was Tuesday . Connors 3rd day at the academy. He was attending his 4th period of the day , which just so happened to be martial arts.Everyone looked at Connor as he stepped up on the mat . Everyone probably thought he was a coward.

Sensei Aia bowed. Connor did the same.

" Mr. Davidson ," He said in a peaceful tone . " You will show the class the ashi barai ,also known as the foot sweep," He walked around the room with his hands behind his back. " This is a very common skill in tykwan doe and you will need to master this in order to beat your opponent. "

Connor shook his head . He adjusted his belt on his white robe and got in his ready position . He bounced up and down on the balls of his feet. **He was ready !**

" Are you ready ? " Sensei Aia asked.

" Yes Sensei ! " Connor shouted.

" Ok then let's begin."

The 2 stood their ground. They gave each other cold blooded   stares . deciding Who was going to make the first move? Connor made the first strike. He threw a fist at Sensi Aia but he was quicker than Connor realized. Sensei Aia blocked the punch with his fists and Before Connor could get out of the way ,was thrown off his feet with a kick to the chest.

" Get up ! You must learn to overcome your weakness and take the pain," the Sensei demanded .

Connor held his side . He took a deep breath and picked himself back up. He wasn't going to give up just yet ! Connor tightened his fists and made his way back to his opponent . When Sensi Aia wasn't looking , he quickly swiped his foot underneath the instructor's ankle . The Sensi was caught by surprise and stumbled to the ground . He lay there for a second, then got back on his feet .

" You lose , " Connor laughed. " I won and you lost."

 The Sensi looked serious .

" You got me there Davidson... you still have a lot of learning to do , but good job ."

The 2 of them shook hands . Connor returned back to his seat.

" Give around and applause for Connor everybody ."

The classroom of 38 students clapped loudly . A smile came to Connor's face .

" Quiet down everybody ..... quiet down ," the instructor hollered. His voice echoed across the room.

Once everybody was quiet, Sensi Aia continued his lesson.

" Now , There are 7 important skills you'll need in martial arts.
 Focus, determination, respect, coordination, discipline, eagerness, and of course confidence . If you don't follow these simple tasks , I believe you will not become a good fighter ."

There was a moment of silence .

" In today's lesson we will be also covering the BJJ , which just so happens to be the greatest self defense technique of all time ."

The students all seemed interested .

" Now there are quite a few moves that go along with this style , such as the triangle choke, american armlock , heel lock, armbar, and the foot sweep which we just demonstrated ". Sensay Aia crossed his arms , making sure his students were still focused .

" As we continue to have class together, we will continue to learn these different moves .... this will take time but if we all stay together we should be able to learn all of these by the end of the year ."

A girl in the back of the classroom raised her hand . The Sensei pointed to her, eggering for her to ask what was on her mind .

" Yes Ms. Lawrison ? Do you have a question or comment you'd like to add to the conversation ?"

The shy girl nodded her head .

" Yes Sensei , I was just wondering if we are ever going to use these techniques in the real world ? "

The young man slipped out a laugh .

" Oh my dear lady, you will be using these skills for the rest of your life !" he said proudly .

" Being a superhero requires lots of crime fighting skills , and that's why I'm here . ...I'm here to teach you how to defend yourself so when you're trying to fight a crook you know how to defeat them ! Get what I'm saying ?"

The girl put a thumbs up , clearly indicating that her question had been answered.

" Any more questions before I move on ? "

No hands went up .

" Okay then ...... we may begin our training !"

....

The rest of the lesson dragged on . The kids were informed to repeat their instructors moves and were given the order to do what they were told. At the end of the class , the students were standing in a single file line where they would have to use their hands to break a wood board in half. Of course Connor was the first in line , so he felt the most nervous out of the group . He walked up towards the board and gave it a cruel harsh stare . He took a deep breath and tried to remember what he had learned . kick , sweap, left, doge : The words repeated in the back of his mind . Sensi Aia was in front of the structure with his hands on his hips . **The pressure was on** . Connor raised his hand up high and sliced the board perfectly in half. Connor gripped his hand and severe pain rushed in. His hand was numb and the color black .

" You're fine ," Sensei Aia called." Get in the back of the line ."

Connor nodded apologetically and went past a group of other kids .
The next contestant stepped up . He was a strong tall boy with black curly hair . He bent his knees and leapt off the ground . He was in the air for a good second , and then came crashing back to the surface with his leg raised high in the air . STRIKE ! The board shattered into hundreds of pieces . There was a shutter of applause and shouts that echoed across the room. Jimm Pearson was one of the best kids in the class and he was already a black belt in karate. If there was one rule you had to follow it was to never mess with him. Unless you wanted to end up with your head dunked in the toilet or get a nasty wedgie. Connor was impressed ! He put a hand to his mouth as he watched the scene before him . How did he do that ?, was the question that remained unanswered . As time went on more kids began to show off their skills . There definitely were a lot of good students in Connor's class period . But as Connor stood in the back of the line , he hoped desperately that one day he would be just as good as the rest of the kids in his class. But he didn't want to get his hopes up , he still had lots of training to do .

" Ok everyone ," The Sensi called to the class, after every one got there turn.

" Class is dismissed. But before I let you go I want to remind you to keep practicing what you learned today and at least go to the gym 3 times a week. Remember , it's on the 6th floor for all you new scholars. They have all the equipment you need and is a perfect place to practice your skills. Understood ?"

" Yes Sensei ," The students cheered .
" Good ...... you now have my permission to leave."

Chapter 16 : kryptonite punch

Sarah looked at herself in the mirror for the 20th time that day . She put on her lip gloss and her pearl diamond earrings, with a red velvet skirt.

" How do I look ?" she asked Rebeca[her roommate] as she twirled around.

 " Beautiful," she replied.

Sarah looked at herself again .

" The skirt just doesn't look right !" Sarah said dramatically. " I look hideous."

" Stop being a drama queen ," Rebecca yelled.

 "And besides , What's this all about anyway ?" Rebeca asked. " Does it have anything to do with that secret boyfriend of yours , Connor?"

Sarah began to blush . She was always nervous when she talked about her crush .

" He's not my boyfriend, we're just hanging out ... you know, like friends ?"

 Rebeca rolled her eyes. " You don't have to lie to me Honey, I know how much you like him. You always stare at him , and dream about him."

 " That's personal , and how would you know ? " Sarah said defensively.

" It's pretty obvious, I always hear you mumbling in your sleep ."

Sarah shrugged her shoulders .

" Well I guess you're right , maybe he is my crush ."

Rebace laughed .

" See i told you , i knew you 2 like each other ….. So what are you doing tonight anyway ?"

Sarah brushed her hair. " We may go bowling or get something to eat ."

"Am I invited ? " Rebeca said sarcastically .

" No silly ." Sarah lightly hit Rebecca on the shoulder. " What I had in mind was the 2 of us being alone."

" How are you going to invite him ?" Rebecca asked.

" I'll knock on his door ."

 " What if he says no ?"

Sarah put down her brush. " He won't say no to the hottest girl in the school ."

Rebeca giggled . " You do make a point."

Sarah pulled out her pocket watch and stared at the time .

" Well I guess I better get going," Sarah said , as she began to pack up her things .

Rebeca turned towards her roommate .

" Alright sis , go enjoy yourself ok ? "

" Of course I will …. oh and by the way, I probably won't be back till 9or 10 ish ."

Rebeca didn't seem to mind .

" Do what you gotta do ," she said calmly .

Sarah smiled and quickly made her way out the door.

....

Connor was still in his pajamas when Sarah came over . He was catching up on some homework from his previous classes , when he heard the knock on his door . He got up from his desk and put on his night slippers . Maybe Frank was going to stop by, Connor thought to himself . But when he opened the door he was surprised to see that Sarah was there ! She looked beautiful and was wearing a fancy red dress . Connor blushed as he looked her in the eyes . Sarah had a big smile on her face , and she seemed like she was in a good mood.

" Hi Sarah," Connor said .

" Hi Connor …. are you free tonight ? " she asked curiously . In the back of her mind she hoped he'd say yes .

Connor thought for a moment .

" Yes I'm free , I just wrapped up an essay for Mr. Hill's class so I should be available for a couple of hours ."

Sarah nodded quietly. " I was thinking if you wanted to grab some food and maybe go bowling ."

"Sounds fun ….. Is Frank and Jessica going to ? " Connor asked , looking out the doorway.

Sarah lowered her face trying to hide her expression . " Actually I was thinking if it was just you and me."

Connor stumbled back in surprise . Had he heard her right ?

" Just the 2 of us ?" he asked .

" Yeah , " Sarah struggled. " Some alone time."

Connors' heart began to beat his chest . He couldn't believe that he was going to spend the night with his crush !

" Ok , can I change really quickly ? … It'll only take a minute ."

" Sure, " Sarah said. " I'll wait out here."

Connor quickly shut the door and skipped over to his closet . He grabbed the finest clothing from his dresser that he could find . He decided on a yellow polo, and brown cacky pants . He didn't want to look like a slob, he wanted to impress Sarah ! After 3 minutes Connor was ready . He combed his hair with some jell before he left .

" I'm ready ."

Sarah smiled gently . Connor looked so handsome that she could hardly lay her eyes off him .

" You look…. Great ! "

" Thank you , you look really pretty ."

The 2 of them laid their eyes on one another for a long moment .Before things could get any further Sarah took Connors hands and 2 of them made their way down a winding staircase. Connor took everything in. The scent of mint and dandelions and Sarah's warm comforting hand. He loved every second of it.   Connor felt like he was living in some sort of dream, his heart was filled with knots of butterflies .

" Why do you look so nervous, Connor ?" Sarah asked out of the blue .

Connor squirmed. " I dunno , I guess I've never held a girl's hand before ."

" You haven't ? Well that's hard to believe."

Connor stopped walking and looked at Sarah seriously .

" Sarah ? I don't mean to be rude but don't you think we're too young to be dating? I mean we're only 13."

Sarah looked surprised .

" Connor, our relationship doesn't gotta be that serious. Just Think of it as a friendship ."

" Right ," Connor agreed. He gripped Sarah's hand tighter.

" Where are we eating ?" Connor added just to change the subject.

" It's called the Heroes Cafe, it's got the best food and serves amazing drinks ! I think you're really going to enjoy it ."

" If you say so ," Connor said sarcastically .

The 2 of them continued on their walk through the school, every so often passing classrooms and waving to ongoing students .Ten minutes later Sarah and Connor entered the heroes Cafe . It was packed with students and teachers sitting down and enjoying their meals.

" You think they still have a table open ?" Connor asked Sarah .

" Let's find out ."

The couple made their way to the front of the restaurant where they were greeted by a young lady . She had orange hair and wore a yellow superhero costume, with a long blue cape .

" Table for 2 please ."

The lady gleamed at her computer screen and looked to see if there were any available seats .

" Why is she wearing a costume?" Connor whispered quietly. " How come on our floor we can't wear costumes ? "

" Because this floor is the only compound in the building where the hero laws of interior aren't banned."

" Can you speak English ? "

Sarah rolled her eyes. " Basically what I'm saying is that the headmaster of the school prohibited the other floors of the academy from using your abilities or showing any representation of your powers. You can only

perform the arts when you're in your classes or in this case, the 12th floor
."

" Oh…. Well that's kind of as stupid law . But Speaking of costumes, why haven't I gotten one yet? I mean what kind of superhero doesn't have a costume ?"

Sarah laughed. " Next week we will have a designer workshop where you will get to design your suit, it's really cool ."

" I'm looking forward to it ," Connor proclaimed .

The 2 of them were cut off from their conversation .

" There is a table available in the back , follow me," the waitress said .

The woman bent underneath her front desk and pulled out a stack of menus . She began to walk to a large booth , Connor and Sarah following behind her . They then arrived at their table. Connor looked around him and took everything in. There was faint opera music playing in the back with candles lit all across the tables. Each customer seemed to be wearing costumes, he then remembered what Sarah had told her. Connor peered in the back kitchen and saw the chef cooking. He had to blink twice or he wouldn't have noticed that the chef actually had 100 arms. Connor also observed that there were flying waitresses taking orders. Maybe Connor was mentally ill or maybe this was really the first time Connor saw real magic.

" This place looks amazing ! I've never seen a restaurant like this before ."

The waitress gave Connor a warm smile.

" Well, thank you ! …. Is there anything you want to drink, or should I give you some more time to decide ? "

Connor and Sarah glanced at each other deciding if they needed more time .

" Can you give us a couple of minutes ?We have to look at the drink specials ," Sarah asked politely .

" Of course, of course, I'll be back in a couple of minutes ," The waitress walked away from the table and instantly flew up into the air . She glided for a few seconds before slowly making her way back to the ground .

Connor stared at the drink menu carefully , trying to decide what he wanted to get .

" What are you getting, Sarah ? " he asked.

" I'll just get a soda".

" How about you?" she added.

Connor pointed to the bottom of the menu .

" This drink looks interesting ....its called kryptonite punch !"

Sarah's eyes were wide open. " I wouldn't get that if I were you", she said seriously ." That drink is way too dangerous ! if you drink that you'll be bouncing off the walls all night . I also heard it can make you fly and do other crazy stuff ."

Infact Connor wasn't afraid of this at all, he was actually quite interested .

" Well I'm getting it Sarah no matter what you say."

" Please Connor ," Sarah begged . "I am warning you ."

Connor swatted his hand at her, applying that he didn't care .

The waitress came soaring back to the table with a notepad and pen in her hand . She landed on the ground and looked at her customers .

" So are you 2 ready to order ? "

" Yes," Connor said excitedly .

" Ok I'll start with you , the new boy ."

 " I'll get the kryptonite punch," Connor said pridefully.

Sarah looked at Connor and nodded her head.

" And you ma'am ?"

" I'll just get a diet coke."

The waitress scrambled down on her notepad. " Want any appetizers to start?" She asked.

Connor and Sarah exchanged looks at each other.

" Sure . What are your specials ? "

" We have the Wolverine blast off burger , the Thor Ribeye steak as well as our famous Beef Bourguignon. It's Superman's favorite ," she added.

Sarah and Connor thought for a moment. "I think we'll split the Burger ."

" Ok , how would you like that cooked ? "

" Medium rare," Connor said . Sarah nodded her head in agreement .

" Ok, your order should be right out." The waitress made her way back to the kitchen. It was just the 2 of them now .

" I wanted to talk to you, Connor," Sarah said . Connor stared into Sarah's deep blue eyes.

" Sure," Connor noticed Sarah fidgeting with bracelets looking concerned and uncomfortable. " You can tell me, " Connor finished.

Sarah took a deep breath. " I don't think I told you this before but I was in a previous relationship with another guy."

Connor gulped. " I understand , " Connor leaned across the table and put his hand on Sarahs. "This must probably be hard for you ."

Sarah nodded her head. " I was very insecure and thought George was overdoing it . He wasn't there for me and never cared about me," Sarah wiped away a tear. " I dunno but I feel like when I'm with you, Connor, I feel like all my worries go away ."

Connors' expression changed .

" I'm sorry you went through all of that Sarah …. I mean I can't imagine what that was like for you ."

Sarah blew her nose into a tissue .

" It's ok, Connor . At least I have someone who truly loves me ," she said.

The 2 of them smiled .

In the distance they could see food coming their way . The large monster with 100 arms stepped out of the kitchen and made his way to Connor and Sarah . He took large heavy steps that shook the entire restaurant, and startled some of the customers . He was holding a large black tray filled with a gigantic hamburger the size of a head ,   the burger was served with a side of freshly cut fries , and broccoli ! The aroma of food scented across the room making Connors stomach churn .

" I have a large wolverine burger with a side of fries and broccoli ," the chef said in a deep raspy voice .

 "Yep, that's us ," Sarah answered.

The chef took a bow and set a stack of plates on the table .

" I think we had a diet coke and kryptonite punch as well," Connor criticized.

The chef put a hand to his head .

" Oh I'm so sorry , I'll get those drinks ready for you.. Is there anything else you need in the meantime ? "

Connor and Sarah shook their heads .

" No thanks ! Just the drinks and maybe a side of ketchup ."

The chef looked confused. " Ketchup ? I've never heard of that".

Sarah slapped Connor on the shoulder. " What my friend meant to say was -can we please have a side of laser beam sauce ? "

Connor had never heard of such a thing ? What the heck was laser beam sauce ?

" He must be a new one aint he , " the chef grumbled. "He is not from our planet.

Connor let out a fake laugh .

" Yeah , sorry about that .... This is my first time here so I don't really know much about the food ."

"Aha , you must be on the 16th floor. All those bloody people ain't teaching you anything . Bet you haven't seen real magic before ."

Connor didn't respond .

" Just messin with you ..... I'll get those drinks ready as well as the laser beam sauce ," The monster quickly made his way back to the kitchen .

Connor's face turned pale. " I almost puked when that guy came near us. He has so many arms, he could play frisbee , read a book, and cook all at once. "

" You shouldn't say that ," Sarah said judgmentully . " We're all family and we should respect each other."

Connor nodded his head.

He grabbed 2 plates from the table , and began to cut the hamburger in half .

" I just want to warn you that the burgers here aren't your typical Burger King type. These burgers are straight from the orchards of Metrophilis grazed by the finest sheep ."

" Wait.... You mean the sheep from Superman's farm ? "

" Yep ."

" Thanks for informing me on that , I'll be extra cautious to see if there's any pink parts. "

"Your welcome ," Sarah disclosed.

A couple of minutes later the chef came back with the drinks and the sauce .

" Enjoy the food ."

The 2 grabbed their drinks and began to dig into their food. Connor added a side of fries to his dish alongside a couple pieces of steamed broccoli .

" How do you like it?"

Connor chewed on his food. " It's rich , it's flavorful, and well cooked. "

Sarah took a sip of her diet coke ." I'm glad you like it."

 Sarah set her glass aside. " you haven't really told me much about yourself …. I mean I know you like reading books and swimming , but other than that you've been pretty quiet about your past ."

Connor dipped his fry in laser beam sauce . " I don't really like to talk about it ."

" If you're uncomfortable we don't have to talk about it."

" No, it's fine , " Connor assured . " It's fine. "

" Well, how about we start off with this …. Where did you used to live ? you know, before you came to the heroes academy ."

" I used to live in Santa Monica. But We had to move to Chicago because of my Dads stupid job."

"What was his job ?" Sarah questioned .

" My parents are both doctors and they had to move here to investigate more about the new virus that's going around ."

" Ok."

"Quick question, can you get sick here ? I mean there's a worldwide pandemic going on around the world ."

" No, the Heroes Academy is immune to the virus; it only can happen to the outsiders, we call them , people we don't have abilities like us ."

" That's cool ! So you're saying I wont get the virus ? "

" Correct ."

Connor thought back . " But wait, 2 weeks ago I had symptoms , I was sick . Why did I have it if you said we heroes are immune. "

" Simple answer… It's because the academy is the safest place to be. When you're a hero and outside of the school barriers, it is possible to pick up the virus . But when you're inside the boundaries , you're well protected. "

" That explains it ! " Connor said .

" Second question, how did you get your super abilities? "

Connor thought to himself for a moment . He could hardly remember how he got his powers in the first place !

" Well…. I don't really know much about my past . I have anger issues and often take medication for it , so I know my anger has something to do with my powers but that's all I can really say ."

" Did you ever hurt someone ? "

Connor took a breath . It wasn't going to be easy to tell the truth .

" Once ," started Connor . " When I was 5 years old, I accidently caused my school to burn. I wasn't trying to do it but I couldn't control it . The good news is that nobody was hurt ,but I could have done a lot more damage. "

" Yikes! !" Sarah said loudly. " I guess your super powers really are more powerful than you think . If you can shoot fireballs out of your hands , and set an entire building on fire I'm pretty sure you'll be a great superhero. You can become famous like superman , batman , and the flash ! "

Connor looked at Sarah seriously. " I don't want to be famous." His voice raised. " God gave me a gift and it's a horrible gift. I wish I was like everyone else ," Connor mumbled under his breath.

" Stop saying that . I Am sick of that attitude, " Sarah argued. " Can we just have a peaceful rest of the night ? …. I don't want to argue with you, Connor, this is supposed to be a fun night out so don't ruin it for the both of us ."

Connor took a deep breath. " I'm sorry , Sarah ….I must have had another outbreak ."

Sarah put a hand on Connor's shoulder and leaned him into her chest .

" It's alright. We all make mistakes in our life, so I forgive you ."

Connor slicked back his hair and returned to eating his food. He had already eaten half of his hamburger , and was starting to get full. Connor opened a straw packet and slid a red straw into his kryptonite punch . He put his lips to the straw and took a big sip . A weird sensation slithered through Connors body . His arms and legs began to shake, and he felt like he was out of control .

Sarah almost choked on her food .

" Connor ! What - what's going on ? "

Connor rose from the ground . " What is happening ? "

Sarah looked at his glass of puch .

" Don't tell me you drank the punch ! Connor, I told you something bad would happen if you drank it ."

Connor was startled for a moment afraid of how high he was in the air ,but then he got used to it .

" This is quite fun … look at me Sarah im superman ! dada dada daaa. "

All the customers turned towards Connor .

" Stop it, Connor ," Sarah whispered. " You're making a scene."

Connor soared up to the ceiling and performed a double front flip . He then did a backflip layout , and came landing softly to the ground .It was like he was floating in space !

He grabbed his glass of punch and chugged another mouthful .

"Connor, I think that's enough ! "

But Connor didn't seem to listen , he was so excited that he completely ignored his surroundings . He was having the time of his life !

" Do you want a refill ?" the waitress asked , floating over to their table.

" I think we've had enough. Connor let's go…. NOW!"

Chapter 17:   The Bully

STRIKE ! The red bowling ball knocked down a set of pins . Connor was up 85 to 65 , and he had a chance to win the game . The winner would get 10 bucks as well as an ice cream cone from sullivans ice cream parlor [located on the 8th floor] . Connor was a feisty player. He hardly dropped any balls in the gutter and almost every turn he got , he got a strike. Sarah was furious! She was very competitive and didn't like to lose, especially to the new boy.

" Hooray ," Connor leaped with joy." I got another strike."

There was defeat in Sarah's eyes . She was going to prove Connor wrong. Sarah picked up a light weight bowling ball and brought it to her chest. She took a deep breath and released the ball . The ball came speeding down the lane knocking down all the pins. Connor was too startled to even speak. The score on the board changed. Connor had 85 points while Sarah had gained another 35.

" How does it feel to be beaten by a girl , Davidson ? " Sarah mimicked .

Connor shook his head. He grabbed his ball from the machine and instantaneously his hands turned to flames. He cracked his knuckles and his eyes were a set of ablaze. Connor threw the ball across the alley and the pins came crashing down. Connor was up by another 40 points.

" Take that ," Connor roared. " That's why you should never celebrate too early."

" You obviously cheated ," Sarah said. " You used your powers to make the ball go faster."

Connor held his hand up in surrender. " Who said that wasn't allowed ? "

" Uhhh ..the Bowling alley policy," She answered stupidly .

The game board shut off , and the lights went dim .

" Well, I guess you won the game Connor," She pulled out a 10 dollar bill from her purse and handed it to him.

" Want to play another Round? "Connor asked , stuffing the bill in his back pocket. " Who knows, Maybe this time you can actually beat me ! " Connor added.

Sarah looked at her watch. " I don't know Connor ... I mean I'd love to play another but it's getting pretty late. We have classes tomorrow and should probably get some rest ,Besides you know how Dr. Sanchez works. He wants everyone in bed before 10."

Connor put a hand on his hip.

" Are you serious ? it's a Thursday night Sarah , besides who says we have to follow the rules ? "

" We're going to be in huge trouble , I am serious ."

Connor slapped Sarah playfully and giggled .

" Come on party popper , let's have some more fun ."

Sarah took a heavy deep breath .

" Ok fine, but just one more game and that's it ."

Connor and Sarah took each other's hands and made their way to the front of the bowling alley . An Italian man was at the desk , suking a cigare while reading the morning paper. He was dressed in a Hawaiian shirt with brown leather pants. The Tv was blasting and in the back a gang of hustlers were drinking liquor and playing cards.

Connor grumbled as he tried to get his attention. The man finally looked up from his paper and he didn't seem happy .

" What do you want ? " he snapped .

Connor put his hands on the counter and looked at the man carefully .

" Excuse me , I don't mean to interrupt but we'd like to play another round of bowling."

The Italian put down his cigarette .

" Another round ? " he asked .

Connor nodded his head and slapped down a 20 dollar bill .

" Yes , we'd like to reserve another lane ."

 The man accepted the money and guided Connor and Sarah to a brand new lane . He then made his way back to his office . Then suddenly these 3 figures appeared out of nowhere. They wore jeans jackets and sharp navy pants. The gang all had greasy black hair and sharp cold eyes. The guy on the left had a cigarette in his mouth while the others were drinking alcohol out of a paper bag. Just before Sarah and Connor could begin their 2nd round of bowling , Sarah's face turned ghostly white. She seemed frightened and tried to hide her appearance . One of the men in the group was a boy named George Mitchel, what just so happened to be Sarah's old boyfriend . The 2 of them dated in their first year , but Sarah quickly broke up with him when he started to act crazy . In the last months of their relationship George would abuse Sarah and make her feel uncomfortable . She hated living this way so she refused to talk to him , and moved on with her life .

" What's up dorks ? " one of the members called. "Ain't it past your bedtime."

Sarah crossed her arms .

" What the heck are you guys doing here ? " Sarah demanded angrily .

The group of boys laughed , but then quickly changed their expressions.

" You better shut your trap lady ! " Another one of the gang members shouted .

" Don't talk to my girlfriend that way ," Connor said savagely .

The boys giggled. George turned towards Sarah. " Don't tell me You're dating this pathetic lunatic."

" He's not a lunatic, George ! And didnt i tell you i never wanted to see you and your stupid gang again ! "

George grinned . " What's wrong baby ? " He teased . " I didn't treat you right ?"

  Sarah tried to ignore him . He took Connors hand and began to push him towards the exit .

" Let's get out of here, Connor , I'm getting sick of these perverts, " she said.

George stumbled back in surprise .

" Did you just call me a pervert ? "

Sarah stomped up to George. " In fact I did , and you deserved it . After everything you've done to me, why should I forgive you ?"

A couple of bowlers stopped their games and stared at the scene in front of them .

George took a sip of booze. " Little miss sunshine gonna put up a fight, don't she know ? You're going to dump me and call it game over , " he cracked his knuckles. " That's not how I play it, little sister. I play it mean and hard , and I'll knock that little goddamn smile off your face."

The Italian man got up from his chair, startled by all the noise .

" Hey stop it you guys ! I'm not going to have to ask you again . You leave these kids alone ," he argued .

Geroges eyes lit up. " Shut up old hag ," Laser beams shot out of his eyes and hit the man square in the chest. " That shall teach you a lesson."

The old man came tumbling to the ground . He dropped down on his knees gasping for breath. Ted [another one of the gang members] bent his head back and in an instant a ball of frozen ice came spurting out of his mouth . The old man was frozen solid, like an ice sculpture. He couldn't move nor talk.
Gasped screams filled across the room . 3 teenagers quickly made their way out the exit , not daring to look back . Almost everyone had cleared out by the time things were getting out of hand .

" Good job Ted ," George said as he gave him a high five .

" Now I say we chase that little boy , and teach Sarah a lesson ! " the team nodded their heads in agreement.

Connor backed up against a nearby wall with his hands raised innocently

.

" Guys you're making a mistake ," he said, trembling with fear .

George pulled out a switch blade and made his way towards Connor. He had no mercy whatsoever .

" Any last words chump ? "

" Don't do it , George ," Sarah yelled. " Please don't hurt him." The gang grabbed Sarah from behind and held her tight, not bothering to let go . One of the gang members came up to Sarah and hit her across the face. Sarah fell to the ground in agony. Just as George was about to stab Connor in the chest , an instant rage of anger swirled through Connor's body . He closed his fists, and rolled back his eyes .

" AAARRRGGHH !!!" A gigantic ball of flame came soaring out of his hands twirling 75 miles per hour . The flame struck George so hard that he went soaring through the air and came crashing into a vending machine . Hundreds of chip bags came flying out, causing glass to spalater across the floor . The other gang members were full of anger and were ready to strike the boy . They wouldn't let him get away with this ! Connor created a flame the size of a basketball and threw it directly at the 2 surviving members. The 2 landed on their backs and were thrown into the bowling lane . They crashed hard into the pins causing an alarm to go off .

" Let's get out of here ," Connor took Sarah's hand and helped her up. They then sprinted out the back exit. After running for 5 minutes straight, they came across a pond. The 2 sat by a tall oak tree panting for breath. It was the scariest moment of their lives !

" Are you alright Sarah ? "

Sarah gazed at her scars and let out a soft scream . The pain was traumatizing and painful.

" I guess... those jerks really know how to put up a fight ."

Connor couldn't disagree .

" We should get going in a few minutes, " Sarah said. " But for now let's relax and look at the stars". The 2 of them laid their heads on the grass and gazed up at the night sky.

The sky was beautiful that night . Stars sparkled in the high moonlight , and fireflies could be seen soaring in the sky . The cool night wind blew against the 2 of them , a moment of silence was sudden .

" I like you, Connor ," Sarah said.

Connor blushed.

" I like you too ."

The 2 of them made eye contact and gave each other warm smiles .

" By the way, thanks for saving my butt out there . What you did was really amazing ."

" It was Noproblem," Connor said, acting like it was no big deal .

Sarah leaned back against the oak tree and put her hands behind her head .

" You know, when I was a little girl I used to love watching the stars . When my parents passed away I felt like the stars became my best friend . They always warmed my heart and brought me joy in the tough times ."

" I'm sorry, " Connor said. " I didn't know you went through all of that."

" Yeah , I'm sorry too ."

Connor probed himself up on his elbow. " I know what it feels like . My grandma is dying from a brain tumor and the doctors say there is no cure," Connor took a mumbled breath. " I guess it's my fault and i can't do anything about it ."

" Connor …. Look at me ."

Connor turned away from the stars and glanced at Sarah .

" I want you to know that you're the best boy I've ever met…. You're not a coward, or a failure, nothing is ever your fault ."

Connor was proud to hear this, no one had ever said something so sweet to him . Butterflies began to swarm in his chest .

"You really mean that ? "

Sarah giggled. " Yes, Connor, And I don't want to wait any longer . I want to be with you the rest of my life. I want to get married , have kids, and live a happy life . So Connor ?" Sarah asked. "I ask you this …. will you be my boyfriend? "

There was a long moment of silence . All you could hear was the buzzing of the fireflies and the sound of a distant wind . So much emotions were building up inside Connor that he could hardly express anything in words . Sarah, the prettiest girl in school asking to be his boyfriend ? This couldn't be real . He grabbed Sarah's hand and nodded his head .

" Yes Sarah , I would love to be your boyfriend ."

The 2 of them sat up from their positions and got up onto their knees. Sarah pulled Connor quickly over to her chest , her arms tucked behind him . Connor put his hands around her too, no longer afraid of what was about to happen . For the first time in his life Connor was experiencing true love . The 2 of them leaned close to one another, their lips gently touching. Connor could feel the warmth and comfort. And he didn't bother to let go.

Chapter 18 : detention

Connor wasn't looking for any trouble, it just sort of happened. But there he was Friday morning, sitting in the principal's office . Dr. Sanchez, the main principal of the school, was very concerned. He was disappointed in Connor and this was his second warning.

"One more strike," He held out a fudgy finger. " And you will be expelled."

Connor leaned back in his chair . " I said I was sorry,"He protested the one millionth time. " It was an accident."

Dr. Sanchez shook his head. " Sorry isn't going to cut it ," his voice raised across the room. " You are in big trouble , young man ."

Connor couldn't express how angry he was . Why didn't Dr. Sanchez believe him? All he was trying to do was save his friend .

Connor crossed his arms .

" It wasn't my fault ," he repeated ." I was just trying to protect Sarah . If it wasn't for me Sarah would have probably been killed ," Connor said.

Dr. Sanchez didn't seem to believe him .

" Look…. You're a good kid Connor , you really are. But you caused damage last night that will cost a fortune ! The bowling lanes are completely destroyed , and what you had done to those boys was out of the acceptable."

Connor put his head down. " What's going to happen to me?"

Dr. Sanchez seemed to give this serious thought. " Well, i could suspend you for 1 week but i have something more better in mind," He toyed with his pen. " Maybe I'll let you do lunch duty ."

Connor gulped. " Lunch duty , sir ? "

" Yes, mister."

Connor was horrified. He wanted to do anything but lunch duty.

" For how long?" Connor asked .

" I'll give you 3 days ," Dr. Sanchez stood up from his chair. " But if you get in any trouble again then I will have no choice then to send you back home. And trust me son,there are way worse punishments than what I am giving you."

The thought startled Connor . He didn't want to return home. He had friends here,   Heroes Academy was the only place he actually felt accepted . Back home a crisis was going on , people were dying from a deadly disease ,and he didn't want to have to live through it all again .

" I understand sir," said Connor hoarsely." I won't let it happen again ."

....

Connor put on a pair of blue scrubs , and stepped into the lunchroom. It was late in the evening so no one was eating yet , but Connor had exactly 30 minutes to clean the cafeteria . He picked up a fluffy moop and soaked it into a bucket of grayish water . He walked across the lunchroom sweeping the floor as he whistled a happy toone . What better way to spend your day on a Saturday? Connor told himself . Frank and Sarah were meanwhile back at the pool drinking smoothies and soaking in the hot tub . Instead Connor was being punished ! It wasn't fair . He was the one always being blamed without reason. How come Connor couldn't fit in like the rest of the students? A group of elderly ladies came walking in from the front of the lunchroom . They were holding boxes of freshly made sandwiches and fresh batches of baked cookies . They were getting ready to serve dinner, which would be held in 30 minutes . Connor wiped a bead of sweat off his face and glanced at the clock . Just 4 more hours of work and then Connor would be free !

Chapter 19: The council

Connor came down to breakfast the next day. The cafeteria was serving thick and fluffy french toast, with scrambled eggs and sausage links. Conor loaded up his tray and sat down on a nearby table. Conor had to sit on the edge, due to the fact that there were over 20 kids. It wasn't the most comfortable !

" Morning Connor, did you sleep well last night ?" Frank asked . He took a bite of his chocolate sprinkled donut .

" No! I was literally up the entire night cleaning the 8th graders mess from dinner."

" That sucks ," Jessica added. " I wish you were with us . We went swimming and got smoothies ."

" Tell me about it," Connor grumbled sarcastically .

Connor saw Sarah looking at him and just smiled. Frank looked at this in awe.

" Wait, are you two are a couple ? Rebeca told me you 2 hung out on Thursday ."

Connor dug into his sausage. " Rebecca must be the worst liar on the planet," Said Connor . Sarah nodded her head in agreement .

Frank put a hand to his chin .

" Hmmm..... I don't believe you guys, I know you're hiding something from me."

Sarah took a heavy deep breath . Frank was always getting into people's personal business .

" Ok if i tell you , you better promise you won't tell anyone ? "

Frank took out his pinky finger and wrapped it around Sarahs .

" Cross your heart ?"

" yes! I solemnly swear ."

" Want to tell him ?" Sarah asked Connor . Connor nodded his head.

" Frank ," Connor looked at him nervously. " Me and Sarah are dating ."

Frank's eyes widened . The truth was revealed !

" So .... You guys really are a couple ?" he asked .

"Shhh ," Sarah whispered. " Everyone's looking ."

A group of teenagers turned away from their plates and stared at Connor and Sarah with their mouths wide open .

Sarah let out a fake laugh .

" Don't worry you guys, he's just making a funny joke, " Sarah implied. "right frank ?" She said, her teeth were tightly gripped together .

Sarah punched his arm and looked at him angrily .

" Right, yeah just a joke ," Frank stuttered.

" He's lying, I saw them making out," one boy called. " He kissed her." He started mimicking kissing sounds. The whole cafeteria burst out laughing. Things were not going as planned ! soon the whole school would find out and it wouldn't go well !

" What do we do ? " Sarah pleaded. Connor and Frank looked around the room nervously .

" I have an idea," Frank said.

" Oh no ," Connor said worryingly. "Frank always has the stupidest ideas ."

Frank got up from his seat and stood proudly up on the table. His hands burst into electricity.

" Hey everybody, listen up ! " he called down. " Or get zapped". He threw lighting balls at the students like they were targets. Kids were thrown all across the room and crashing into objects. " Make it stop , they called. " We're sorry."

" I'm just having fun ," Frank laughed.

After 3 minutes of panic and fear , Frank closed his eyes and everything was back to normal.

" Who wants more ? " Nobody answered. Some were hiding under their desks while others were already out of the room.

" Good, because if I hear any one of you talking about my buddys behind their backs," Frank had hatred in his eyes , " Then I swear I'll make you suffer worse ."

The kids gulped in scardness . There was no more time for goofing around so they started to continue on with their meals .

 Frank turned back towards Connor and Sarah . " Problem solved !"

The assembly took place at ten thirty the following afternoon . Thousands of students gathered into the gym where the head principal Dr. Sanchez was making an announcement . Today he was dressed in a black tuxedo with a red bow tie. His hair was slicked back in a polite manner, and a handkerchief was grasped in his hand . He wasn't wearing his usual superhero costume as he always did . He took a deep breath and stepped up to the microphone which was displayed on a large stage .

" Ummm ,ummm ," he cleared his throat, as he tried to get his students' attention .

" Everyone listen up please, I have a very important announcement to make ."

The students' laughter died down.

" Thank you…. Now if you do not know already there is a deadly virus spreading across the world ! Millions of people have already been infected and the cases are continuing to rise by the week ."

Students gasped. Clearly alot of them weren't paying much attention to the outside world .

" The man behind this is John Mcdell ," The principal hit a button and a picture of him flashed on the projector . " He is 75 years old and is a well known scientist . He got his degree in music and arts in 1963 and even opened his first million dollar company right after college. Mr. Mcdell was a child prodigy at an early age ," The next picture on the screen showed him at age 10 playing on a piano. " He could play Mozart's symphony N0.40 blind folded and could memorize every Shakespeare book. Mcdell got all A pluses in all his classes leading him to be Harvard's top student ."

A Lot of the students were impressed , including Connor ! This man definitely was interesting , Connor thought to himself .

" John was also a great scientist ! He invented things that changed the world and was nominated for over 100 nobel prizes in his lifetime ! but there was also a dark side of John .As he grew older he was no longer a happy man , in fact he had somehow turned evil . As time went on he hardly left his office . He spent the last decade trapped in his laboratory making potions that he hoped would destroy the world."

Dr. Sanchez paused for a moment .

" It wasn't until a couple of months ago when we discovered that Jonathan was working on a new invention ! An invention that would cause chaos and disaster." He clicked on a new photo, this time of Jonathan working in a science lab.

"From our research we can claim that he is the mad man behind this terrible crisis . He and his evil company have been poisoning food products all over the world, causing more people to get this virus and making this disease spread 10 times faster ! News reports have been filed and everything is getting out of control."

Connor hated the sound of this . He wondered if his parents were safe back at home, or if they had also catched the virus . Whether the news was he just hoped his family was ok .

" But Dr. Sanchez, why haven't the police authorities arrested him yet ? you clearly have evidence that you can show them ," an african american student asked .

The principal rubbed his palms together and looked at the student seriously .

" Look, thousands of reports have been filed in the last number of months . But you have to understand that Jonathan McDell is not an ordinary crook . He isnt easy to find . He lurks in the shadows, and resides out of the public eye . It's nearly impossible for anyone to track him down . Tons of investigations have been going on but I'm afraid there's really nothing else they can do ."

The student nodded his head and sat back in his seat . It wasn't easy to accept the truth .

" Now I know what you're all thinking ," Dr. Sanchez began ." You're probably wondering how this has anything to do with you ."

Dr. Sanchez leaned closer into the mic. " Well let me tell you this . 3 students will be sent on a mission to break into Mcdells science headquarters where they will have to bring back a sample of his secret antidote . If all goes according to plan , we can find out what chemicals Mcdell is using and find out how to stop him from creating more of these substances ."

Connors' heart began to beat in his chest . Deep down he wondered if he would be called to participate in this mission . It seemed like a pretty tough job, having to sneak into a laboratory and get past a crazy scientist ! He didn't let the thoughts overtake. There was a 50 % chance he may not even go .

"I have a shoe box here . In this shoe box there is a list of random names in which I will be calling ." Dr. Sanchez showed the class the box . He then looked away and began to shuffle the cards around. He then picked out 3 random note cards.

" The first contestant we have is ...Sarah Robinsion ," There was a round of applause from the students. Connor tapped Sarah lightly on the back. "Congratulations," he whispered . " Thank you ," Sarah mouthed.

" Moving on to our 2nd contestant , please give a warm welcome to Frank Tremblay ."

There was even a louder set of applause. " I can't believe it ," Connor said to Sarah. "First you and then Frank ," Sarah chimed in. " The cards must be marked. It can't be a coincidence that the 2 of you randomly got chosen."

Connor wondered if he was going to get chosen next . There was definitely a possibility ! He crossed his fingers.

" And now for our 3rd and final contestant ." Dr. Sanchez pulled out the final slip of paper and examined it carefully .

The pressure was on !

There was a moment of silence . Dr. Sanchez was shocked by what he was about to read.

" Well folks it looks like our final hero just so happens to be …. CONNOR DAVIDSON !" His voice echoed through the building.

The whole room turned their attention towards Connor . Everyone looked at him and was surprised he had gotten chosen . There were a thousand other kids at the academy that were braver, stronger, and more powerful than him . They couldn't believe that a small 13 year old boy was chosen for such a deadly mission .

" This must be a mistake, " Connor pleaded.

" Yeah ," one of the boys protested. "How can this loser be chosen? I'm way cooler , watch this," The kid closed his eyes and levitated from the ground. " See," he called. He sat back down.

" I can dodge bullets ," another called.

" I can read people's minds ," a third chimed in.

" All this freak can do is cook ." The whole class burst into laughter. Connor felt like he wanted to hide in a hole.

" I know all of you have incredible talents, I really do . That's what makes you all unique.   But you all have to listen to me ! I don't make the rules around here ok ? I withdrew a random number of cards and it so happened to be Connor , and I don't have control over that !Connor was chosen for a purpose and he must embark on this quest no matter whether you like it or not ," Dr. Sanchez finished.

The whole room was silent.

" Do I make myself clear ? " he shouted.

" Yes , sir ," they all moaned .

" Ok . How this is going to work is our 3 contestants will leave tomorrow morning no later than noon. They will break into Dr. Geniuses' facility and try to bring back the serum . The rest we will handle ourselves. If our heroes manage to survive then their mission is accomplished ."

Dr. Sanchez walked off the stage , proposing everyone to follow his lead . The assembly was now over and classes were about to begin………

Chapter 20: costume design

Connor was stumped for the 50th time that day . He had spent almost all afternoon cursing to himself and throwing away loads of paper . He sat in his dorm room that night, trying to decide on what he wanted his superhero costume to look like.   All of the other first year students in his grade had already designed their suits including Frank who had been bragging about it all week long . Of course Connor barely had any knowledge on designing and hardly knew where to start. All of his ideas were too simple and dumb in most cases . Connor glanced at the clock .It was 9:30 pm indicating that Connor only had 30 more minutes to finish his design ! Everytime he glanced at the clock he became more and more nervous . After a moment of hard concentration an idea finally came to him . An idea that was better than his previous ones . He quickly sharpened his pencil and began to sketch on a clean sheet of paper . He drew in as much detail as he could and tried not to make any mistakes . He wanted his costume to look perfect ! Connor drew for almost an hour when he had overcome the decision that his sketch was ready ! He held the sheet of paper over his desk lamp and glanced at it carefully . The picture was shaded in bright red alongside features of yellow. There was a long cape drawn to the back of the suit , as well as a rubber mask . On the chest area a red fireball logo could be seen .

"Perfect !" Connor thought to himself quietly . " This is exactly how I wanted it."

Once Connor was finished he walked over to his computer and opened up Gmail . He took a screenshot of his costume design and sent it right away to Dr. Sanchez . Tomorrow morning his suit would be completed ! Connor was beginning to feel tired so he decided to head to bed . He had been up for almost the entire day and he needed rest for tomorrow's mission .

Connor put the piece of paper back in his folder and turned off his desk lamp. He then took off his clothes and changed into his pajamas. Connor slid into bed and pulled the sheets over his face . He closed his eyes. But It was hard for Connor to sleep that night. He kept tossing and turning and would have these terrible nightmares. Connor was scared about tomorrow. He was about to go on his first mission. Connor kept thinking to himself if he would ever make it out alive. There was probably a low chance of surviving. Connor also felt a sense of guilt for leaving his parents. They were probably worried sick about him. But even though Conor liked it Here , it still didn't replace home. Home was his house in Chicago. It wasn't The Heroes Academy. He wasn't born here or raised up here. He didn't have the intention to feel like he belonged. Maybe Connor was better off being a normal kid. Maybe being a superhero wasn't the best choice. Maybe everyone would be happier if he wasn't around...

Chapter 21 : Break In

Genius headquarters was a run down building where few passers would expect to find it. The sanctuary itself was over 20 years old and locusts and ants were starting to inhabit it . All across the building hundreds of security cameras were in focus . A tall electrical wired fence was surrounded across the territory , as well as patrol guards who never left their positions . Jonathan never wanted anyone to get inside his lab . He was a very private man and often kept his work a secret . Connor knew the job wasn't going to be easy ! There were dangerous obstacles he had to pass in order to get in , and he didn't know if he could get through them all. He had just started at Heroes Academy only 2 weeks ago and now he was being sent on a mission to save the world . When he was a little he always dreamed of being a superhero . He'd run on the kitchen table with a red blanket pretending he was superman . He put out his arms and pretended he was flying just like the hero he grew up reading about. Of course he was a kid at the time and hardly knew anything about the reality of being a real one. Connor closed his eyes and didn't let the pain over tak him. He had to do this for his friends and family. He wasn't going to let them down.

" Are you ok?" Sarah was concerned and could tell that Connor wasn't telling her something. " What's wrong ? "

Connor looked at Sarah. " I-Am Sc-ared ," he stammered , the words barely coming out . " What if we don't make it ? "

Sarah tapped Connor on the shoulder. "Everything will be ok," There was pride and content in her voice." Everything will be fine."

Frank joined in on the conversation. " First things first, how do we get in ?"

The trio had been trying to work this out the whole morning. They thought of every single possible solution and were still stumped.

" Why don't we try the back ?" Frank asked . " Maybe there's some sort of secret entrance to get inside ."

Connor and Sarah looked at Frank trying to decide if this was a good idea. There could possibly still be tons of guards blocking the back , but there was a chance there maybe was another entrance .

" That's a great idea ! But let's split up so we dont look suspicious ... There's still tons of security cameras so we have to do our best to stay out of view,"Sarah exclaimed .

Connor and Frank nodded their heads . They had finally formed a plan !

" Everyone huddle together ."

Sarah and Frank formed a circle around Connor .They all put their hands together and looked at one another .

" Alright everyone, let's give this our best shot . We know it won't be easy to get inside this lab but we all have to have hope . Jonathan will do whatever it takes to kill us ,but we can't let that happen ! We have to do our best to make sure no one spots us alright ?"

" Yes."

" Sure thing ."

Connor smiled . He was glad he had friends who actually cared about him.

" Great ! Now Sarah, you head towards the left, Frank you go to the right, and I'll be behind you guys . Stay low and remember what we learned ."

The group backed away from one another and got in their positions . They adjusted their capes and masks and made sure they were ready . There was no turning back now, their mission was about to begin !! Sarah tiptoed to the left and tried her best to stay out of sight . After a few more steps she rolled on the grass and layed on her stomach, just like she had learned in training class . The grass was wet and her costume was clearly stained but she didn't have time to worry about it .She began to crawl slowly on her elbows , making sure she wouldn't be spotted by any security guards . Meanwhile, Frank was headed the opposite direction and was already halfway towards the back entrance . Connor was behind them following Frank and Sarah's lead , and making sure the coast was clear . So far everything was going as planned . As Connor and his friends turned a corner they suddenly came to a stop . In the distance Connor could spot a gang of guards in yellow jumpsuits with oxygen tank masks . They were holding large rifles by their sides.

" Guys , it looks like the back entrance is guarded as well,"Connor started. " What else are we going to do ?"

Sarah looked up ahead .

" I'm not sure... all of the other locations are either locked or have guards surrounding them ."

" She has a point, " Frank chimed in ."I mean if this is our only option I guess we just have to try our best to get past the guards ."

An idea formed in Connors head. It was probably a stupid idea but it was the only one he had. " Guys listen , I have an idea. Maybe we should knock the guards out with our powers."

"I think that's a great idea," Frank said.

"Terrific thinking,"Sarah rejoiced.

"Alright then ... let's kick some butt !"

....

The 3 uniformed guards didn't move. They held their positions with their rifles slung across their shoulders, alert and aware of any bypassers.

They looked across the territory , high alert for anything unusual . But what they didn't know was that a group of superheroes were lurking in the distance, ready to attack ! Frank was the first to react. He used all his instincts and shot lightning out of his hands. One of the guards was zapped and collapsed to the ground instantly. He wasn't moving and could hardly breathe. The other 2 guards stumbled back in surprise, unsure of what had just happened . Then out of nowhere another attack was made ,This time by a young teenage girl. She moved her arms in a circular motion causing a huge wave of water to come spurling out of her hands . The water had so much force that it made both of the remaining guards fallback . Frank ,Connor, and Sarah didn't have much time to admire their handywork, because they only had a limited amount of time before the alarm went off and more troops came. Connor walked up to the guards making sure they weren't moving . He formed a fireball with his fingertips and blasted it at the men for extra precaution . He took a deep breath and walked a little closer , Sarah and Frank following him from behind .

" Are they dead ?" Frank asked .

Connor looked at the guards closely .They were all smoking ,and severely burned. Connor had really hurt them badly.

" I think so... I mean they're not moving ."

" That's good," Frank proclaimed.

Connor rolled his eyes. " 2 down and 500 hundred more to go ."

Sarah got on her knees and flipped over one of the men to his side . She zipped open his coat pocket and carefully took out a red key card. It had a barcode on the bottom with an old picture . Connor , Sarah and Frank then stripped off the guards clothes and put it on . They were going to disguise themselves as guards , it was the easiest way to break into the compound.

" We got the key ! Now we just have to pretend we work here and steal the samples ," Sarah exclaimed .

Connor and Frank nodded their heads. " Alright", said Frank." Let's make this quicker than it has to be ."

The 3 heroes quickly put on their yellow jumpsuits , looking left to right making sure no one would spot them . Once they were dressed [which took forever] They walked towards the entrance in a fine manner and pretended everything was normal . They used their ID cards to unlock the door and then made their way to the laboratory.

" So far so good," Frank whispered.
The heroes entered the laboratory and admired their surroundings . They could see hundreds of scientists in white lab coats working with all sorts of chemicals . Fire erupted across the room , as well as green gasses that smelled horribly disgusting . It was good they had oxygen masks on. A few of the scientists locked eyes on Connor and his friends , but did not pay much attention to their entrance . Frank gazed across the room in amazement . He kept on the lookout for any bottles or samples that looked out of the ordinary . Finding the antidote was going to be harder than they thought !

" What should we do you guys ? There's so many things inside this place it's almost impossible to tell what we're actually looking for ," Frank said.

" You're right . You think we should go checkout the 2nd floor? Maybe we'll find something up there."

The heroes agreed on the decision, and began their journey up to the 2nd floor . They climbed a winding staircase while passing more scientists and men in yellow jumpsuits . Frank passed a vending machine and stared at it for a few seconds . Of course Connor , and Sarah didn't have time to buy food so they quickly pulled Frank away . They then reached an office which was located in a deserted hallway. The front door read : `Jonathan mcdell` .

" This must be his office," said sarah.

" He must be gone ," Connor acknowledged. " But we probably don't have much time ."

" I agree ," Frank said. " Mcdell may not be here now but he'll most likely be back soon ."   Connor turned the knob of the door and they entered the room. The hero's first thought was that Jhonathan was not a well organized person. Stacks of paper were scattered everywhere , his desk was toppled with books and computers, and it seemed like everything didn't have a real meaning of care . Connor and his friends tiptoed to

Jonathan's desk , where tons of drawers were aligned with one another. They scanned through all of the drawers looking for the antidote . So far all they could find was more paper and lab sheets .

" Look what I found ," Frank was holding up a trophy. " This was the reward John received in 1978."

" Put that down ," Sarah hollered. " We're not supposed to be touching stuff."

Frank put down the trophy. " This is like an ancient museum. I bet some of this stuff is worth thousands, even millions ."

" It's no time for finder keepers Frank, we're on a mission and we have to stay focused."

" Right ," said Frank apologetically .

Just when Connor was about to give up he spotted a small bottle tucked away underneath Jonathan's desk . Connor reached out and grabbed the bottle and jumped up with excitement !

" Guys, I think I found it ! " Connor cried .

Sarah and Frank looked away from their exploration and gazed at what Connor was holding .

" Is that the antidote ?" Frank questioned .

Connor admired it and a smile came to his face .

" This has to be it ! It perfectly matches the description Dr. Sanchez gave us."

Frank took the vial from Connor's hand and studied it for himself . He looked at it closely and was quiet for a moment .

" Sarah , I think Connors is right . This definitely is what we're looking for, " he said proudly .

But then they were caught off guard . In the distance they could hear loud booming footsteps making its way down the hall . With no doubt they knew it was Jonathan Mcdell or one of the guards ! Connor panicked as he looked around the room . He didn't know what else to do. If Jonathan entered the room and saw that Connor had one of his samples he would go insane ! Without hesitation, Connor grabbed his friends by the hands and ran towards a supply closet. The door then creaked open and a man stepped into the room. He made his way to his desk , looking around the room for any suspicion that someone was here. Connor , Sarah and Frank's heart was beating quickly. They kept their mouths shut not squeaking a single word. It was hard for them to see much, the tiny crack in the door blocked out most of their sight . Jonathan sat on his chair and dialed a phone number. He picked up the receiver and started to talk.

" Everything will be ready soon," a dark cold voice called out. " The antidotes will be set by next Tuesday, and let the rest do the talking." Connor , Sarah and Frank could hear the voice vaguely on the other end. He sounded french and stern. Jonathan, still with the phone in his hand, walked over to his cabinet and poured himself a glass of scotch. He leaned back in his chair and took a sip.

" I understand Mr. Rodriguez. The money will be financed to you immediately ."

The voice on the other end replied back and it didn't sound happy . "JONATHAN ! I don't have time to wait around ... if you want to keep making antidotes and keep your company in business then you need to fulfill my wishes ! Do you understand ? "

Jonathan set down his glass and put up his feet .

" This is some sort of misunderstanding sir . I told you I'll get you that money but you need to believe in me," Jonathan stammered .

There was a scream on the other end as well as the sound of shattering glass .

" Fine.... I'll give until thursday but if you don't - "

The man's voice was cut off .

"Relax , relax, relax, everything will work out perfectly ." Before anymore could be said Jonathan hung up the phone and walked out the door .

Connor was breathing heavily as well as Frank who was having a panic attack . Frank was claustrophobic and was always afraid to go into tight spaces . Sarah on the other hand looked like she was about to faint .

"You guys alright ?" Connor whispered .

The 2 of them were clearly petrified .

"That was the scariest moment of my life, " Frank said .

Connor opened the closet door an inch and looked out into the open . No one was in the office . Just before he was about to step out he felt a strong force pull on his jumpsuit .

" Wait , are you sure he left ?" Sarah commented .

Connor looked at his friends bravely and nodded his head .

"Yes Sarah , I heard him leave ."

Connor stepped out of the tight space and gestured for his friends to follow him . Sarah and Frank hesitated for a moment but once they got a look for themselves they stepped out as well . The room was just as they remembered it , papers everywhere and hundreds of lab sheets . Connor took off his oxygen mask and threw it to the side . His face was covered in sweat and it was hard to breathe . Sarah and Frank followed his gesture and caught their breath for a second . Their mission was halfway completed , but the hardest part was yet to come .

" How do we get out?" Frank asked.

Connor looked out the window. "We jump ."

" Are you serious ," Sarah argued. " That's a pretty high drop. If worse comes to worse we will break our leg or neck."

Connor ignored Sarah and opened the window shill. " Are you coming or not?"

Sarah and Frank were frightened . Jumping out of a 2 story building wasn't what they had planned on doing.

" You're crazy ," said Frank." If you think we're going to listen to you , then the answer is no!"

" It's the only option ! All the other escape routes are being patrolled by guards . If we keep wasting time we're going to get caught ."

Connor walked towards the window cill and peered down at the surface below him. He took a deep breath and leaped ! He felt the cold air rush against his face , as well as the death defying sound of the wind . A little more than 5 seconds later, Connor came splurging to the ground . He rolled into a summersault and landed on his bottom.

Sarah was too shocked to even speak. " Connor," she called. She ran over to the window and peered down. " Connor, are you alright?" Connor was lying on his butt on the grass, but he didn't seem to have broken any bones. Connor put up the thumbs up sign , signaling that he was OKAY.

" I'm alright ! " Connor called up to his friends ." I'm fine."
Sarah and Frank let out a heavy sigh , they were so glad that Connor wasn't injured .

"Ok Sarah you go next …. don't be afraid, just believe in yourself and everything will work out ."

Sarah stepped up to the windowsill , her knees were trembling and her hands were shaking uncontrollably . She tried to remain calm but panic was taking control of her .

" Don't look down ," Connor reassured. "Just jump."

Sara took a deep breath and leaped off the platform. She screamed in mid air, her arms flapping like a bird. She was in the air for a good 2 seconds before she landed in the grass. Sarha came tumbling down ninja style, and landed perfectly back on two feet. Sarah and Connor shared a laugh . They both gave each other hugs , glad that they were both alright . Meanwhile, Frank was still on the 2nd floor .

" Come on Frank ," they called . " Don't be a scaredy cat."

Of course Frank was afraid of heights . Ever since he was a little boy he hated riding on escalators and climbing tall trees. But now he had no other choice. It was either jump out of the window or let the bad guy win !

" Just give me a second ! " he called out .

Sarah put her hands to her face." You have fought ten foot monsters and got struck by lightning, and you're telling me you're scared of heights. For pete's sake."

" I told you I hate being high up !"

Sarah put a hand on her hip and looked at Frank sternly. Clearly she wasn't happy .

" We don't have much time … Jonathan is going to be back soon. Now are you coming or not ? "

Frank stared at his friends for a quiet moment . Finally he had enough . He realized that for once his friends were right , he needed to trust himself and get past his limits !

" I'm coming down !" Frank called .

Sarah smiled and gestured for Connor to step away and give Frank some space .
  After one final deep breath Frank bent his knees and leaped out of the window . He performed a double frontflip , then a gainer backflip right before he came crashing to the ground . Connor and Sarah put their hands to their mouths . They couldn't believe Frank had just attempted something so dangerous !

" I -i-i-… I DID IT !" Frank shouted happily . " That was much easier than I had expected ."

Connor put a hand to Frank's back and gave him a gentle pat .

" Nice job !"

" Yeah , that was incredible !"

A smile came to Frank's face .

" Thanks you guys, " he said proudly .

Connors' expression softened. " Guys, I think we have more trouble." He looked nervously behind him. Six patrol swat members were making their way toward them.

" Duck ," Connor ordered. The 3 dropped to the ground , sparks of bullets ricocheting over their heads. They moved on their hands and knees , mud dirtying their trainers and uniforms. An alarm rang through the facility , red lights flashed. Connors first thought was that Dr. Genius found out that someone was in his office and stole the serum. Without thinking Connor shot up from the ground and instantly shot a ball of flame out of his hands. Before he could get out of the way a gun bullet was fired towards his head . He jumped behind a small rose bush in a stage of panic . He could have died if he wasn't fast enough !   The fireball spread across the grass of the facility causing a large wildfire to spread around the guards .They were trapped and had no escape . They were literally burning alive.

" Awesome , dude ," Frank called." Now it's time to show them what I really got." Frank closed his eyes and volts of electricity flowed around his body. He threw his hands at the guards, electrocuting all of them. They fell to the ground, shaking and unable to move. " Hey , What do you call 3 electricuted guards?" Frank smiled." Toast ." He threw one more bolt of lightning at the team , and they were dead instantanaly.

Before their celebration could continue another army of guards appeared in the distance . This time they looked stronger and tougher than the previous ones . Clearly this wasn't going to be an easy escape !

" How many more are there ? " Connor said dreadley.

Sarah stared at them in disbelief. Clearly she wasn't expecting this !

" Let's make a run for it ," Connor concluded." Are powers are already dying down and we are getting tired."

Frank and Sarah agreed on the decision , they didn't want to spare another moment of their lives . The 3 heroes got up from the ground, and picked up speed running the fastest they had ever ran in their lives . More gun fire was shot causing destruction all around . The 3 ran for cover, their hands shielding over their faces . They then leaped across the tall wire fence with all of their strength   and were greeted by a fast speeding vehicle coming down the road. Dr. Sanchez was sitting in the driver's seat with his foot on the pedal . He waved his hand gesturing for the heroes to get in the car .

"HURRY UP !! THERE GETTING CLOSER !" He demanded ,his face as red as a tomato. The 3 opened the car doors and slammed them behind them. The vehicle picked up speed and soared through the air. The army of guards watched up in amazement as the car soared into the distance . The men smashed their weapons to the ground in disappointment , the good guys had gotten away !

"This car has wings?" Frank said, astonished. " That's epic."

Dr. Sanchez chuckled .

" There's a lot of things about this car you don't know ."

Frank's eyes gleamed in excitement . " It's like the flying car from Harry Potter."

Sarah laughed along. " It sure is ." The vehicle passed a foamy cloud.

" Do you 2 have the antidote ? " Sarah asked."Don't tell me you forgot it. We risked all our lives to get it ."

 Connor fished the bottle out of his back pocket. " Relax guys, I have it here, there's no need to worry ."

Sarah wiped a bead of sweat off her face , she was relieved that nothing bad had happened to it .

" Thank goodness ! You almost gave me a heart attack , " she said .
 Dr. Sanchez speeded up the engine a little faster and continued on his route. He had a GPS attached to the front steering wheel where a set of instructions were displayed .

" According to our tracking system we should get to the academy in about 5 minutes . Traffic is a little bit backed up , but I'm sure we should get back in time for lunch, " Dr. Sanchez instructed .

Frank's stomach grumbled . He was clearly hungry and couldn't wait for a fine meal back at the academy .

Sarah opened up a book and put on her headphones from her bag . She leaned back in her seat as she enjoyed the calming flight .**That was a close one** , Connor thought to himself as he rested his head on the car seat . He had a rough journey and really needed some rest . He closed his eyes and before long wandered off into a deepless sleep.

Chapter 22: Security footage

" How in the world could you let them escape ?" John McDell rasped. "How did they get away?" he slammed his fist on the table , knocking down papers and books." You had a job , Sergeant Filmroe and you disrespected me."

The general looked scared and nervous. " I'm sorry , sir ," he stammered . " I won't let it happen again."

Jonathan reached in his desk and took out a revolver." No .. you won't." He pulled the trigger , The bullet hit the general right in the center of the chest . General Fillmore dropped down on his knees and dropped to the floor. He laid still, a pool of blood surrounding him.

" That shall teach you a lesson," he said quietly under his breath . Jonathan then picked up a phone and began to dial. He contacted the Removal team to take away the body.

" We have a dead body in room C-304," Jonathan spoke into the receiver. "We need someone to take it to the dump," He put down the phone. A couple of minutes later a team of 10 men in green suits entered the office . They put the body in a garbage bag and exited the room. A little while after, Jonathan had called in another Assistant into his office. His name was Sir Francis, and he had worked at Genius Headquarters for over 20 years now. He wore black neon boats, with a tall brim cap, and a cameo uniform . His hair was greasy and dark and he had a long unshaven beard. He also loved smoking. He would smoke up to 2 packs a day. Because of this, he had a low hoarse voice and a bad whooping cough. The commander also smelled like booze and smoke, which was always lingering from his uniform.

" Commander."

General Francis saluted and shook hands with his boss . " Good to see you Mr. Mcdell."
 Francis was greeted warmingly to his seat, and he accepted.

Jonathan sat behind his desk, fidgeting with his ring on his left finger . " I need to talk to you ," He looked at Sir Francis with contentment in his eyes. " It's very important ."

" Yes , sir ," Sir Francis responded. " I'll take pardon for anything you have to say," He took off his cap and rested it in his lap.

 McDell leaned back in his chair. " General Francis, I was reported last night that 3 tennagers had broken into the facility and had stolen one of our samples from the lab ."

" That's correct , sir ."

" Well..... do we have any idea or possibly who these 3 vigilantes could have been."

Sir Francis seemed to give this thought. " No , sir ," he replied quickly.

Jonathan sized up his assistant. " And why is that , General? Did I not give you strict orders on being fully ascertize on your part."

" No sir ," he gulped nervously.

Mr. Mcdell got up from his chair and slapped The general across the face. Sir francis flinched , putting his hand on his left cheek.

" Don't play smart with me ," John hollered." I already killed One of your people and it makes me wonder if I want to do the same to you."

 The general held his hands up in surrender. " There must be a misunderstanding , sir."

Mr. Mcdell took a deep breath and sat back in his seat. " Sorry for the inconvenience , let alone me hitting you." Jonathan greeted his commander back to his seat , and Francis obeyed his order.

" Doctor," Francis sutured after a long period of silence. " Is it possible we can look at the security footage?"

Jonathan's eyes lit up. " That's it ," he jumped to the conclusion." You're absolutely right," Jonathan snapped his finger. " Screw me for me being so stupid," He patted his assistant on the back. " Go get me that footage ."

....

Jonathan plugged the hard drive into his laptop. He clicked on his mouse and hit the play button. The video had a time stamp on the left corner and the time read, 12:45. At this moment in the video , 3 tenneagers in masks and tights were running through the compound. Jonathan hit his space bar and zoomed in on the image. It was hard to make out any faces but Jonathan could see pretty well. There were 2 boys and 1 girl. Jonathan had to replay the video multiple times to spot the green antiotide in one of the boy's hands. Jonathan jumped to the conclusion right away that this boy and his so-called gang were the prime suspects. There was no question about it .

" General, Francis ," Mr. Mcdell called.

The commander came barging into the room. " Yes, doctor ?"

Jonathan set his glass of whisky down. " Can you tell me who these kids are ?"

" Sure thing boss ." Sir Francis walked over to the computer and began to peck the keys. He did a full photo scam and did lots of research. After 5 minutes , Jonathan was getting impatient.

" Well ? " Jonathan said , in an angry tone ." Who are they ?"

" I did a full body scan sir and found out these 3 are superheroes from the Heroes Academy ," Francis punched in more keys." The one on the left is Connor Davidsion, otherwise known as Fire boy. He has the ability to shoot fire out of his hands. The person on the right is Sarah Robbisnsion," he zoomed in on the picture." She is also referred to as Water girl and has the ability to control water. When she was just 7 years old she was on a cruise and the boat went overboard. She managed to escape but her parents were not so lucky. We then have Frank. He's a fat chubby kid who loves nothing more than eating. His superpowers are strength and determination. He is also Electric and can cause lightning storms when he's at his full potential. My theory, doctor , is that these 3 broke into the compound in order to steal a sample of our serum for experimental purposes. They heard about the world wide virus so they decided to find out the secret behind it all. They're going to go back to the academy and run some tests. Once they find out our ingredients they can run this company out of business. So what are we going to do ?"

Jonathan bit his fingertips. " We're going to Kidnap the girl." There was fire in his eyes. "Then we will kill the boy and his foolish gang of superheroes." He took one last sip of his drink. "They'll pay….. Big time. They should've known that no one messes with the doctor !"

Chapter 23 : The lab

Frank adjusted his goggles as he slipped on a white lab coat . His hands were covered in white hospital gloves alongside a paper mask covering his mouth and nose . Sarah and Connor were beside him already straight to work .

" Frank, can you pass the stirring rod ? " Connor demanded calmly as he held a beaker in his hand .

Frank ran over to a nearby tool box and peered inside . There were dozens of pieces of equipment packed together that it was so hard to tell what equipment was what .

"Umm.... For some reason I can't seem to find a string rod in here ? "

Connor grumbled under his breath . He clearly had a long day .

" Frank, for the hundredth time the stirring rod is underneath the funnel ! If you actually paid attention you'd see it ,"Connor argued .

Frank wacked his head with his forehead pretending to play dumb .

" Oh ! My bad ," he said as he now found what he was looking for . He grabbed the rod and passed it over to Connor . He quietly said thank you and got back to work . Connor leaned over a large magnifying glass and peared at the antidote sample . It was green and began to squirm around the table . Sarah stumbled back from her seat , nearly knocking down a display of pitchers .

" THAT THING IS ALIVE ! " She screamed as she pointed at it with her finger shaking nervously .

Frank ran over to the table to see what the commotion was about .

" Sarah what's going -."

He couldn't finish his sentence . He leaped up into the air and ran around the room like he was being chased by a dog . Connor was just as surprised as his friends were !

" Calm down you guys everything is going to be okay, " he said almost out of breath.

Sarah covered her mouth and began to cough rapidly . She ran over to a nearby dress can and began to barf . Connor knew he had to do something but he had to make it fast ! He looked across the laboratory trying to spot anything to keep the moving substance in place . So far all he could see was dozens of cylinders , funnels, viles, and cabinets filled with loose papers . This was the only sample from Jonathan's laboratory that the heroes had , and if it got lost they would be doomed ! After one last search Connor had finally found something that could work . He grabbed a glass cup that was displayed by a faucet and as fast as he could made his way back towards his table . He put the cup over the substance instantly right before it was about to leap off the counter. He took a heavy deep breath and put a hand to his side . He was winded and needed to catch his breath for a moment . Frank and Sarah stopped their crazy behavior as the moving substance was put behind the glass .

" What in the world just happened ? "

Connor didn't know what to say . This was new to him just as it was to his friends .

" I-i- I don't know ! I think the antidote is a living organism or something . Whatever Jonathan is doing with these samples is incredibly dangerous ."

Sarah couldn't agree less . The mad man was clearly up to a severe scandal .

" So what do we know about this antidote ? " Frank asked .

Connor rubbed his chin and admired what was in front of him .

" Well, we know it can clearly move on its own , but what do you think Jonathan is doing with all these samples ? "

Sarah pulled out a stack of newspapers from a supply cabinet and laid it infront of her friends .
" Well, there's been hundreds of newspapers that have been published in the last month and they're all related to this new virus ."

Sarah flipped to a random section in one of the papers where a large headline read : **Death rates rise !**

 " In the past month People have been getting food poisoning all around the world . There's been reports from local restaurants and food industries that people are getting sick from these food products !"

Connor put a hand to heart in shock !

" Oh yeah , I remember Dr. Sanchez told us that ! " he exclaimed .

Sarah nodded her head . "I know right ? "

"Anyway , I think Jonathan is somehow using these samples to poison these foods which is causing the virus to spread ! "

"So what do we do next ? You think we should contact the authorities ? He's clearly doing illegal stuff, " Connor questioned .

Sarah shook her head .

" Connor, you know how powerful Jonathan is ! He owns a million dollar company and he could easily win a court trial. He could pay a whole lot of money to clear his name, " Sarah said .

Connor slapped himself in the face realizing that for once Sarah was right. They authorities could not win againsts someone like Jonathan, he was like the king of England !

" You're right …. I guess it's up to us to stop this fiasco . If the police and court can't do anything about this then we will. No matter what the risks are or the dangers we face, we will do whatever it takes ! "

Chapter 24: The phone call

Connor awoke the following morning . He had large bags under his eyes , and his hair was a Bird's nest . It was Saturday , one of Connor's favorite days of the week . He had no classes that day and often spent his time hanging out with his friends . However, at a little past 5:00 am he was awoken by the presence of Frank . Frank was wearing Power Ranger pajamas with a stuffed Teddy Bear by his side . At times Connor felt bad for Frank, he seemed like he was 5 rather than 13.

"Connor, Connor , Wake up !" he shouted, as he began to tug on Connors blanket .

Connor was still for a moment enjoying the comfort of his bed when all of a sudden he was startled instantly . He leaped off the bed and screamed in a stage of panic .

"Frank, what are you doing here ! Do you have no idea what time it is ?" he questioned .

Frank's face was full of sweat and he looked nervous and worried . From the look of things Connor knew something wasn't right .

" Connor you have to listen to me , it's about Sarah …. She's gone missing ! " There was contentment in his voice and it sounded scared and worried.

" What do you mean she disappeared ? But She was with us last night," Connor inquired .

" I don't know, I went to go check on her this morning but her bedroom was empty !"
 Connor shook his head, he couldn't believe what Frank was telling him ! " If your playing a stupid prank on me , l swear ill kill you."

" Iam serious , " he stuttered. "I'm not lying."

Connor put his hands over his face and began to pace around the room. His girlfriend was missing and no one knew where she was! The world was getting crazier day by day .

"So what do we do now ? We can't just sit around while she could be getting killed for pete's sake ! "
Frank noticed that Connor's temper was getting out of hand . He walked up towards him and put a hand on his shoulder .

"Connor, please calm down . I'm sure Dr. Sanchez will know where to find her. I mean she couldn't have gone too far, " Frank protested .

Connor shook his head back and forth .

" Frank, you don't understand ! If Sarahs is missing, there's a high chance we're never going to find her."

Frank took a seat on Connor's bedside and took a heavy sigh . He was out of ideas.

" You're right , I guess there really is nothing we can do ."

The truth was too hard to accept . Connors bright proud face began to disappear and soon tears and sadness took over . Connor couldn't believe that this had happened ! It felt like he was living in some sort of nightmare that he was dying to wake up from . But after every minute passed he knew he was living in the moment , a time he wished to escape .

" Who-who would do such a thing ? Sarah has done nothing wrong."
Connor took a deep breath and then proceeded on. " I don't know what anyone would want with a young teenage girl ."

Frank sat by Connors side. " It's all my fault," he wailed. "I didn't share the leftover pizza with her ."

Connor looked at Frank awkwardly. " Buddy, I don't think it was because of that ."

Frank looked at Connor ." Really?"

" Yeah, i'm One hundred percenet sure."

" Then where is she?"

Connor put his hand on his chin. " Maybe she was kidnapped ."

" Or abducted," Frank chimed in. " By an alien."

" Not helping Frank ."

Frank shrugged his shoulders. " I give up ."

Connor tucked his knees into his chest. " We can't lose hope. We can't ."

The 2 sat there in silence. The sun beaming through the drapes, and the soft chime of the clock ticking. They didn't speak a word. Then out of the blue the phone rang.

The 2 stared at each other. " I wonder who that could be ?" Frank and Connor leaped up from the bed and made their way to the kitchen. Connor picked up the receiver .

" Hello? "

" Hello , Connor ," the voice on the other end replied.

Connor was star struck . How did this man know his name? "How do you know my name?" Connor questioned. " Who are you?"

" I know many things about you," the voice was cold and sharp like razor knives ."I know where you live, I know your favorite color, I even know where you are right now."

Connor was scared. He and his friends could be in huge danger. He had heard of scammers and petifilers. He also knew to never talk to strangers. Maybe there was an instinct in Connor to put the phone down and walk away, but Connor couldn't. It could be about Sarah. He needed answers.

" Who are you ? "Connor repeated.

" Iam many things, Connor. I Am your worst nightmare, the devil, the unknown, the monster who hides under your bed. But what I really am is a Scientist . A mad scientist who wants to over run the world. I Am the one and only Dr. Genius, the civilized man who seeks to control power and wealth amongst thousands of innocents. I seek to forbid my people to kneel before me and sacrifice themselves amongst the eternity of god. And I will.. Time will only tell."

Connor was lost for words. " You ," Connor snarled." You caused the virus that's killing thousands of lives."

" Yes ," the voice muffled. " That is me ."

Connor couldn't process all of this . What he had been told was that this man , who he was talking to, was responsible for the death of thousands. He should've known.

" Where's my girlfriend you creep ? " Connor demanded , his palm tightening around the receiver .

A cruel evil laugh echoed across the line .

" Questions, questions, questions, that's all you ever ask ."

Connors' anger began to take control and before long he was as hot as a fireball .

" Answer my question ! I know you've done something to her ."

Dr. Genius was quiet for a moment.

" Indeed I do have her."

Connor gasped in disbelief. " you little scrum bu-."

" Now now,"Jonathan interrupted tantidley."Play nice , boy . I wouldn't argue if I were you . Your little girlfriend is locked up in a cellar, and if you contact anybody or tell anybody," he warned. " I will find out and kill her. Do you understand ? "Jonathan shouted.

Connor wasn't afraid . Jonathan was nothing but a crazy scientist who wanted nothing but revenge . He didn't scare him one bit no matter whatever little plans he had up his sleeves .

" I'm not afraid of you Jonathan ! You hear me … im-not-afraid-of-you!! I will hunt you down and stop whatever selfish schemes you're planning to do . You're nothing but a crazy scientist who has a crazy mind ! " Connor yelled aggressively .

In the background out of nowhere Connor could hear muffled cries . They sounded frightening and in need of help . Connor knew it had to be Sarah! Connor tried to hold back tears . He hated hearing his best friend sound so frightened .

" Connor ," the voice boomed. "I think you also have something for me. It's my serum . I'll make you a deal. If you give me the veil I'll spare your girlfriend. Deal ?"

" How can I trust you?" Connor asked.

The voice was quiet for a second. " You just have to ." The phone went dead.

" Who was that ? " Frank asked, sitting on the counter munching a glazed donut.

Connor put the phone down on the counter. " Dr. Genius ."

Frank almost dropped his donut. " You mean Jonathan Mcdell the mad scientist ? "

" Yup, and he doesn't seem happy. He's angry and wants to make a deal."

" What's the deal ?"

" He wants me to give him the sample in exchange for Sarah ."

" You can't do it ," Frank pleaded. " You can't."

" Sarahs in danger Frank."

" I know but if Jhonathan gets his hands on the serum, he can destroy the world."

Connor took a breath and looked at Frank .

" I know,but we can't just let Sarah die ! She's our friend dude and we have to stick up for her ."

Frank finished his donut and wiped his hands on his shirt .
" I think it's time we tell Dr. Sanchez about this . We can't just keep this a secret ! "

" You're right . Let's get going before anything else gets out of hand ."

Frank smiled. " I heard they have mints in the office."

Connor rolled his eyes. " You and your food."

" They also got those jalapeno popcorn and chocolate chip mi- ."

Connor put up his hands trying to stop Frank from proceeding on .

" Frank, I promise once this is all sorted out we can have a nice lunch at Wolverine Cafe alright ? "

Frank thought to himself for a moment and then smiled .

" Sure , I'll have a double wolverine burger with cheese an-."

" Not now silly … I meant After our work is completed . "

Frank shrugged his shoulders. "Ok,"he said disappointedly.

Connor played along . "I got a gift card for later so we can get as much food as we want but for now we have to stay focused."

" Hooray ," Frank leaped up."Unlimited food ."

" But Frank, we have to do our job first . That's our first priority. When we're down we can then celebrate and eat ."

" Fine ," said Frank as he crossed his shoulders."But let's make this quicker than it has to be ."

Chapter 25: A warning

Connor and Frank told everything to Dr. Sanchez the following afternoon. They told him about the phone call and how Sarah was practically missing! Of course the head director was interested in what the 2 had to say but he still wasn't fully sure if they were telling the truth . They also informed him about Dr. Genius and his evil plan. They left out minor details but mostly told the truth. But for some reason Dr. Sanchez wasn't buying it.

Dr. Sanchez leaned back in his chair as he took a sip of dark brown coffee.

" So tell me…. When did you notice that she disappeared ? "

Connor took a deep breath and pointed towards Frank . " This morning I was in bed and Frank came barging in . He looked really nervous and worried and he told me that Sarah was not in her dorm room !" he exclaimed .

Dr. Sanchez added a pouch of sugar in his cup. " Do you have any idea why she could have gone missing?" He stirred his coffee. " Did you aggravate her in any way , where she could have felt eager to run away ?"

Frank pounded his fist on Dr. Sanchez's desk and stood up in his chair .

" We did nothing wrong, mister ! We are her friends, we would never hurt her in our life !"

" Yeah , why would you blame us for something so cruel?" Connor chimed in angrily .

" Settle down now you two ," the principal instructed. " You don't need to raise your voice."

Connor and Frank sat down back in their chairs. " Can you help us ? "

Dr .Sanchez gave this thought. "hmm...., " he stroked his beard. " I will try . But for the benefit of the doubt, it was your responsibility , Especially you," he gleaned at Connor ." You say she disappeared but who would take her? The Heroes Academy is the Safest compound in the United states !"

Connor couldn't argue . He knew fighting wasn't going to solve anything !

" Listen to me .... I know for a fact that Dr. Genius is behind all of this . In Fact he was the one who created this deadly virus in the first place ! This morning he even called me and told me he had Sarah ."

Dr. Sanchez almost spit out his coffee at the sound of Sarah's name .

" Wait, did you just say Jonathan Mcdell kidnapped her?"

Connor nodded his head in agreement .

" Yes sir, that is what I have been trying to tell you ."

Dr. Sanchez cursed to himself and grabbed Connor by the hand .

"Why didn't you tell me this earlier ! If Dr. Genius has her; it means there's a high chance that she's not coming out alive ."

" I'm sorry - i- I was afraid you wouldn't believe me . But it's too late to dwell on the past now we have to go find her ! " Connor said .

Dr. Sannchez put his coffee down on the countertop and leaned in towards his computer . He shifted his position in his chair and tried to get comfortable . Connor and Frank walked towards where he was seated and peered at the screen in front of them . The head director quickly pulled up a tracking website where he searched in Jonathan Mcdells name . Over a dozen results popped up all implying hundreds of different people who were named Jonathan . Dr. Sanchez scrolled down on his mouse for a few seconds until he found the Jonathan he was looking for. On the screen a younger picture of the mad man was displayed showing him in his mid 40s with a white lab coat secured across his body . He looked handsome and not the kind of person who was soon going to destroy the world !

" Perfect ! From my research and best amplification it looks like Dr. Genius is located in some sort of cave ! "Dr. Sanchez zoomed in on his screen as he looked closely at the image before him . " It's huge and - and- I see Sarah ! She's trapped in a prison cell ! " he exclaimed .

Connor took a close look for himself and indeed Sarah was trapped in a cave ! She looked pale and skinny and seemed like she had lost quite a few pounds . Connor hated seeing her look like such a mess .

" This is horrible ! Dr. Genius is not treating her right ." Connor walked away from the computer and made his way towards the office exit . " We gotta find her and get her out -."

Before Connor could proceed on, a large medal lock clicked into place .

" I'm sorry Connor but I can't let you go on your own ! You're only a boy and a mission like this is too difficult for a young hero like you ... I'll call up the whole school and we'll all do this together as a team ."

Connor walked away from the door realizing it was no use . He had to follow the head director's orders no matter if he liked them or not .

"Fine, but make it quick we have to save Sarah before it's too late ."

 As if on cue Dr. Sanchez quickly ran over to a large intercom that was connected to all levels of the school. The headmaster slicked back his hair and adjusted his bow tie . After a big deep breath he walked up to the mic about to make his announcement . Time was ticking and he needed to be quick . He put the speaker towards his mouth and leaned in closely .

" Attention all students ! Attention all students ! Everyone please report to B-209 and get your superhero costumes on quickly . Danger has risen and I need every single one of you to get prepared for battle ! "

Connor looked out the office window and over a dozen kids were already on the move . They ran across the halls like they were being chased by zombies and made their way towards B-209 .

" I inform you to bring your weapons and gear, and get changed quickly. We don't have much time ," Dr. Sanchez instructed over the intercom . "Everyone please meet by the nearby dock located by the beach , from there we will sail across the ocean and make our way to a deep deserted cave on the other side of the canal. Please follow my instructions and be ready in 5 minutes. Thank you ." Dr. Sanchez put down the speaker.

 Connor turned towards his pals. " Vamos amigos. We have a long journey ahead."

Chapter 26: the cave

The ship sailed across the icy waters, waves splashing and a strong storm brewing. All the members of the Heroes Academy were aboard a huge cruise ship that was over 20 feet wide ! They had been traveling for almost 2 hours now , and the night grew windier and colder by the hour . Fishes and sharks manifested the oceans and stingrays and fish were hiding amongst the surface. It was a stressful day for the heroes , they were being sent on a mission that was deadly and dangerous . In the back of their minds they wondered to themselves if they would make it out alive . Saving a kidnapped girl trapped in a cave was not an easy task . Dr. Sanchez steered the boat towards the right avoiding a flock of whales and making way to the oncoming island up ahead . The island was a mile away from where they were sailing. The island had long narrow rock faces with tall trees and sand. It was hard to make out every detail, but they got the clear image. On deck over a hundred heroes were leaning on a tall rail . They glanced at the still ocean watching the amazing sealife gleam before their eyes . All of the heroes were injected shots before the adventure, due to the virus which was at stake. They were the safest in the academy where they were immune, but the outside world was dangerous, so they had to stay safe. The caped crusaders were hidden amongst the shadows and their stomachs dropped when the boat carried further. All of them had discussed and went through the plan, multiple times. Their plan was that they would trick Dr. Genius into taking a fake sample of the serum , then they would grab Sarah and quickly make their escape. If all went according to plan they would pull off phase 2. Phase 2 was when they would blow up The Genius Headquarters laboratory and stop more deadly virus samples from Being made . It seemed like a lot. They all knew that a few sacrifices would be made. If 100 heroes died to save the lives of millions, then that's how it would have to be.   The waves began to churn as the boat began to board the upcoming dock . Tiny schools of fishes could be seen swimming in the shallow ends munching on seaweed and swimming around in circles . Large sand dunes were spotted up ahead as well as a large open cave where Sarah was being held prisoner ! Connor hated the look of it . It sent shivers down his spine just knowing that his best friend was in there . The boat came to a sudden halt , and all of the heroes were directed one by one to step out. They did this single file and made their way to the awaiting cave. Their boots crunched against the pebble rocks , and high winds began to pick up . The smell of garbage lingered throughout the cave walls as the heroes made their way inside . Connor lit his hand to light the way , and proceeded through the darkness with his team behind him. Frank obviously was scared of the dark ,so he trotted behind Connors back. Connor gleamed across the rocks and spotted hairy spiders and other nasty insects.

" Hello," Connor's voice echoed through the cave." Jonathan ?"

There was no answer . Everything was quiet and dark.

" It's Connor . We have the syrm . Just come out and we will give it to you ."

Then suddenly a tall figure appeared out of the shadows. A robotic figure stomped its way into the cave opening . Jonathan Mcdell was wearing the suit with a happy smirk on his face .

" Well if it isn't Connor Davidson and his little team of superheroes ," he smirked. " You just made it on time . One minute late and I would have killed your little girlfriend ."

" Where is she ? " Connor demanded.

Dr. Genius chuckled. " Give me what I want and she's all yours ."

Connor put his hand in his left pocket and carefully pulled out the fake antipodate . It was time to trick Jonathan !
Dr. Genius' eyes lit up and he licked his lips . He finally had what had been taken from him ! Connor walked up towards the mad scientist and placed the antidote in his palm . Jonathan glanced at it for a second wondering if anything was usual about it .

" This better not be a stupid trick of yours ."

Connor now became nervous, what if Dr. Genius found out ? If he did Sarah was never going to be saved . " No s-ir ," he stammered. " Why would I do th-at ?"

" Because ," Dr. Genius started ." I know all of your selfish tricks ."

Connor looked around the cave. He needed to find Sarah quickly, but first he needed a distraction. Dr. Genius still hadn't bought it, but they still had to make their rescue quick and efficient .

Jonathan stepped closer to Connor. " You lied to me . This is a fake. The liquid is green , not blue ."

Connor cursed to himself quietly and smacked his head with his palm . He was so stupid ! Of course the antidote was green , when he snuck into the laboratory last week he saw what it looked like . He was in such a rush in the past week that he hadn't had time to pull off a realistic serum !

" Please,"Connor pleaded , holding his hands up in surrender. " Don't hurt her ."
Connor knew he was doomed . Sarah was never coming back to Heroes Academy ever again , and it was all Connors' fault .
Dr. Genius' face began to turn bright red and his eyes began to widen . The heroes had never seen a man look so crazy in their life !

" You just made the doctor very very angry !" he smacked the veil to the ground, glass shattering everywhere ." And you should have known at the start , to never mess with me."

Connor quickly turned towards the large group of superheroes and looked at them desperately .

" Alright guys ,"Connor whispered." You all look around the cave and find Sarah. And I'll keep Dr. Genius distracted. Are you ready ?"

A muffled cry of shouts echoed through the cave. Connor turned back towards Dr. Genius with his hands ready by his side . His heart was beating fast, his palms began to sweat, this was Connors final chance to redeem himself and save his friend !

" Prepare to Die Boy. I gave you a choice and you spat it back in my face. But now you must learn the hard way ." Dr. Genius threw his first punch , throwing Connor hard into a pile of rocks. Connor lay there motionless. All of the air was sucked out of him and his ribs felt like they were broken. Dr. Genius stormed up to Connor and kicked him in the face , Connor screamed in agony. " You're nothing but a weak , pathetic little boy ." Dr. Genius threw another punch , hitting Connor square in the nose. His nose was bleeding and he was coughing up blood. Connor felt defeated . He felt hopeless . He felt like he for once did not have a chance against the villain .

" What's wrong? Is your little team of friends not gonna save you ?" Jonathan said in a taunting tone .
Connor lifted himself up from the ground, the pain lingering through his body . But right before he could stand on his feet, again he was kicked right in the face ! His jaw made a loud snapping sound and 3 of his adult teeth fell out from his mouth . Blood was dripping across the corner of his lip with a sudden urge of pain ! Connor needed help , he knew he couldn't defeat Jonathan on his own, he was just too powerful . He needed his friends , he needed Frank and Sarah , he needed all of the help he could get .

Dr. Genius lifted his metal foot and stomped on Connors arm.

"Ahhh ," Connor screamed, the cruciating pain taking over. He rolled to his side, gribilig his arm in agony. His wrist was dislocated in an awkward position .

" Looks like I've already won."

Connor looked up at Dr. Genius, Connor's vision was fuzzy." I haven't given up yet ," he spat. " And I never will."

....

Meanwhile the superheroes were teamed up into 2 different groups . One team was searching toward the left , and the other was searching towards the right . They ran as hard as they could, dying not to waste a second of their time .

" We're almost there ! let's keep on the move, " Frank demanded .

The cave was a living maze . Every corner would turn into a dead end and it seemed like the heroes were going nowhere, but they couldn't give up just yet !

" I've heard about something like this," one of the heroes called. His name was Night rover. " It was called the Labyrinth . And in the Greek myths, the labyrinth was a confusing maze where at every twist and turn you would end up at where you started."

" We don't have time for a history lesson, " said Jessica, trotting behind him. " We have to find Sarah before Dr. Genius finds her. And I don't think Connor can distract him much longer ." The masked figures kept on running, their legs were burning and they were out of breath . They didnt know how long they had been traveling for but they knew they had been running long enough . Then suddenly they heard screaming coming out of the other side of the cave. The heroes came to a sudden halt.

" I think I hear someone," said Frank. " Quick ," he directed. " Let's move left."
A sudden hand gripped Frank from behind before he could travel any further . An older man who must have been around 17 with a long green cape peared at Frank closely .

" I don't think we should go that way, " he stammered .

" And who are you ? " Frank asked. " Some sort of GPS system. What gives you the right to indirect my lead?"

The man put his hands on his hips and stood proudly .

" I am known as the one and only compass man, a hero who is great at giving directions ! "

Frank nearly choked laughing. " Compass man ? " He put his hand on his knees , he was laughing so hard. " So what , You're like AGPS ? "

" Yes, that's exactly what I am , and according to my knowledge it seems like we are heading in the wrong direction ."

" So we go left ?"

" Right ."

" Right? "

" No , Left."

Frank put a hand to his head." You just confused me."

Compass man let out a chuckle and cleared his throat ." What I am trying to say is that we must travel to the left. There's nothing towards the right except a dead end that will take us nowhere ."

Frank nodded his head, now fully understanding what the hero was instructing .

" Great ! Then we'll follow your lead mister know it all ." The group headed toward their new direction and came to a sudden stop . Up ahead they could see a large prison cell that was held on top of a high structured cliff face.

" Holy cannoli ," Frank swore." That's Really high ! " He looked up at the cliff face. "How the heck are we going to get up there ? "

" We climb, " one of the superhero members replied . The girl's name was superjestic cat girl . She wore a back superhero outfit with a yellow cape tied to her back , and a logo of a cat on her chest .

" Easy for you to say ," said Frank. " You're a cat. You can climb. And besides, I'm not doing it . If you don't know, I have a phobia of heights."

" Really ?"said the Compass Man . " I didn't know that ."

" Yeah,"Frank shrugged his shoulders. "Go ask my psychiatrist."

Compass man put his hands on his hips . " If we're all too scared to get up there then there's physically no way we're going to save the girl . It's either we're wimps or we climb that cliff !" he instructed .
Frank shook his head hating the idea . He really had no other choice.One by one , the heroes were instructed to climb up. It took almost 20 minutes to complete the whole range and it was also very tiring. It was also hard to get a grip on the rocks. You would have to hold onto the rocks with your

fingertips and hope you wouldn't fall down. The rock face was also very steep and narrow. A fall from this high would certainly kill you. More than 50 other heroes flew up towards the top, while the other 100 weren't so lucky . There were times Frank wished he had other superpowers , and in this moment he wishes he could fly . It would really make a difference .

" Don't look down , don't look down," he told himself. After a long journey to the top , the group finally made it to the top of the tall structure . It was a breathtaking journey and everyone had no energy by the time they had finished . Lucky for Frank he had actually packed a few cliff bars so he provided some to a couple of the heroes who needed them . For a couple of minutes the superpowers decided to lay it low . Frank leaped in joy, doing the rocky dance.

" Yo Adrian ," he called, lifting his hands up high and pouncing on his balled feet. " Yo Adrian ," he shouted again, using his best Silvester Stallone accent.

A few of the members chuckled. But before long they were off and about once again . They proceed on the route having to pass some tall structures , a few manholes , and lastly some deadly spiders which Frank was scared of . " Did you know I also have arachnophobia?" he blurted out. The group just shook their heads. They didn't have time for any more stories . Then suddenly they came across a metal cage. A short fragile girl with light strands of hair , was sitting inside.

" There she is," Frank whispered. But to his disappointment he saw 3 uniformed guards beside her. "Shoot ,"he cursed to himself. "We got Officers."

" That's not good ," Jessica said.

" I have an idea," one of the heroes called. He had dark skin and was wearing a white costume with white boats and a cape." My power is to turn invisible so I get past the guards and grab Sarah . You guys can stay put
"
.

" Great idea ," the heroes all agreed. " Terrific thinking ! "

" Ok, i'll be back ." The Invisible Boy put on his cloak and he instantly vanished. He crept past the guards, careful not to make a sudden sound. The 3 officers who were guarding the cage were wearing navy blue uniforms with tall jackass boats. Rifles were slung by their side , with cigarettes hanging out of their mouths . The invisible boy crouched down low and made his way to the men. He was going to scare them away . He snuck behind one of the guards and pulled off his top hot.

" Ahhh," the guard screamed. " A ghost." He ran around in circles with his hands up in the air. The other 2 guards saw the floating hat too . They almost jumped out of their pants , and ran as fast as they could away from the compound. The invisible boy had to hold in the laughter that was coming out uncontrollably. He lifted the hat up and dropped it to the ground. From 50 feet away , the other heroes saw all of this. They were laughing and excited. So far the plan was going as planned. The Invisible Boy then made his way to the cage. He pulled off his hood , revealing his true self. He came up to the metal bars and peered inside. Inside there lay a skinny girl, tucked in a little corner. She was wearing a torn up blue costume with blood trickling down her face. She seemed scared and alone. The Invisible Boy tugged at the bars, but they wouldn't budge. He tried tugging , and pulling but it was useless. Then an idea formed in his head. Maybe he could fit through the bars. It was a tight squeeze but it was the only option he had. He stepped through the bars , tucking his head in his chest. He squeezed through the narrow gap , and to his surprise was in the cage. He walked towards the corner where the lost girl was sitting.

" Hey ," he called, and the lonely girl looked up . " I am here to help, don't worry. I won't hurt you."

She backed away an inch." Stay away from me, creep ." She shielded her hands over her face.

The Invisible Boy took a breath." I was sent from the Heroes Academy. I'm with Connor ." The mention of that name startled Sarah instantly. She leaped up from the ground and bear hugged him.

" You found me ."

" Yes."

Sarah leaned in closer." How did you find me? "

" We tracked you ."

Sarah wiped a tear from her cheek. " I was so scared and worried …. I -I ," she couldn't bring herself to say it . " I thought I was going to die ! "

The invisible boy chuckled and took the girl's hand . " Yeah, we were all thinking about you. I'm so glad you're ok ."

" Where's Connor ?"Sarah asked, looking around the room.

The superhero took a heavy sigh and slumped his shoulders . " Sarah, to tell you the truth, he's in the middle of a fight with Dr. Genius ."
Sarah clutched her heart and her breathing began to pick up pace .

" No …. No …. This -this - this can't be happening ! Connor's going to get killed ."

The hero nodded his head but quickly changed his expression .

" I know it's hard to process but everything will be ok . Anyway, we have to get going. We gotta get you out of here before more guards come. Connor can't buy that much time. He's trying his best to hold him off but he can't hold him up forever ! "

" Ok ," Sarah whispered." Let's go. "

Connor Davidson was knocked out for the 100th time that day . He was like a punching bag, constantly getting punched at . He would get hit so many times, and continue to fall to the ground. Connor must have broken every bone in his body now, and the pain was obserk. Connor wasn't mentally or physically strong enough to beat Dr. genius. But as Connor lay there , motionless on the ground he just hoped his friends were coming to the rescue .

" Are you finished yet ? " Dr. Genius started. " Do you give up ?"

" We don't have to fight …. Lets just sort this out, " Connor said .

Dr. Genius laughed. " I gave you a second chance, And You blew it all away. If you just cooperated with me, none of this would have ever happened ."

" Shut up Jonathan ! You're nothing but a crazy absorbed scientist . Why can't you just stop all of this . You can change your life around and show the world that you really are a good guy ."

" I will never change ," he raged . " The world is nothing but a cruel dark miserable place . Ever since I was a kid I was bullied and harassed. Do you know how hard that was for me? "

Connor gulped . "Just because you were bullied doesn't mean you're not the only one. There's millions who are bullied , I can help you . We can help you. You're making a mistake. Killing millions of lives is doing more harm than good."

" You don't know the other side of the story. I created this virus for my haters. The people who bullied me. I Am doing it for revenge. Every action has a consequence and they need to pay."

" You're killing innocent people. Not everyone is bad Jhonathan. Think about it . You creating this virus isn't solving anything . You're creating more enemies and more monsters . Is that what you're Really want? . A world full of destruction and chaos. Just use your head for once. This isn't you. I know you're better than this. You just have to believe me."

" You're wrong," Dr. Genius spat. "Iam right and you're wrong ."

Then out of nowhere Connor could hear footsteps . They were fast paced and were making their way towards the cave entrance . Connor turned his head and noticed the sighting of over 100 superheroes running towards him . They were back from their trip and they were not alone . In the middle of the group Connor could see the outline of a cute girl in a blue superhero skirt . Without hesitation Connor knew it was Sarah ! She had finally been saved and Connor had never felt so happy in his life .Just as Connor was about to make his way towards her he felt himself being pulled back by a sudden force .
" Not so fast ! You seriously think I'm going to let you escape from this cave with your little selfish friends?"

The heroes stopped in their tracks with fear and disbelief . Getting out of the cave was not going to be as easy as they planned . Connor tried to squirm away from the mad man's grip but the force was too strong .

" You see friends, this is what happens when someone does not obey my orders !" Dr. Genius shouted .

" Put him down Einstein ," Frank called savagely. " Put down my friend ."

" Yeah, you psycho, "another hero called out from the back . " Let him go ."

Dr. Genius dropped Connor . Connor came hurtling to the hard cold ground, his head hitting the concrete.

 Dr. Genius cracked his knuckles.

"Want to fight heroes ? Then show me what you got !"

The superheroes adjusted their capes and masks and got in their ready positions . The battle was on !

" Heroes ... ATTACK !!! " The army of Heroes leaped up from the ground and began to attack. Shields and spears were thrown, while balls of flame and ice came hurtling from the sky . A few of the heroes flew up towards the cave walls shooting surprise attacks and dodging bullets from Dr. Geniusis robotic suit . So far the Heroes seemed to be in the lead. They were winning, and they were undefeated. Connor got up from the ground slowly rubbing his head and stood on the balls of his feet . He was ready to fight again ! Connor took a breath and then back his head and curled his fists together . He felt the rising heat form on his fingertips and a sudden urge of anger . Connor lifted up both his hands and in an instant a ball of flame the size of a beach ball orbited around the room . It spun for a few seconds right before slamming directly into Jonathan's suit. Frank snook behind Dr. Genius and bolts of electricity shot out of his hands. Dr. Genius fell to his knees, in agony . The mad man was down and it was finally their chance to make their escape !

" Everyone, let's get a move ! Someone grab Sarah and follow me back to the boat ," Connor ordered . The heroes grabbed Sarah from her position on the ground and made their way outside the cave. Connor threw one last ball of flame at Dr. Genius and followed the rest of the crew. Jonathan was out cautionious but it wouldn't be long before he would wake up and be back on the chase .... By the time the crew had made it out of the cave it was raining hard . Thunder rumbled in the distance, and floods of water rushed in.

" Get to the boat ,"Connor yelled . " We have to make a run for it ! " The crew ran towards the large cargo ship, the rain splashing on their costumes. The heroes stopped in front of the ship a little while later and step by step, proceeded up the side ladder . When they reached the top they made their way to the engine room. Dr. Sanchez was alerted by the opening of the door, and turned his back away from the wheel.

" Are we ready to get going ? " he asked. " It's been almost an hour."

All of the heroes were out of breath . "Hit the wheel .... Now ! " Connor said as he clutched his side . Dr. Sanchez glanced at Connor carefully . " Are you alright you seem like you really - ."

" Just hit the wheel ! We don't have time for any explanations. Just take us to Genius headquarters , I'll explain the plan later ."

" Alright ," Dr. Sanchez pulled back the engine . " Fasten your seatbelts ." Dr. Sanchez hit the gas and the boat chopped along the waters. Wind roared in all of the members' faces. The boat was going at around 50 knots an hour, and it was already far far away from the tiny island. Before the crew could sit down and enjoy the ride any further,something was spotted in the rearview mirror of the passenger's seat . Dr. Sanchez glanced at it carefully and his mouth dropped . In the distance he spotted 2 speed jets racing along their side. They must have been the officers from the cave.

"Uh oh- looks like we have trouble," said Sarah. "Don't worry, I'll take care of this." The young girl moved her hands in a circulatory motion and closed her eyes and concentrated. Then suddenly the currents began to rise . She lifted her arms up higher and summoned a tidal wave that spread quickly across the ocean surface . 2 of the boats came splurging into the water as the large force of waves hit them from in front . A series of gun fires were launched but the bullets were missing the targets. The huge wave came splashing down, throwing the guards underneath the abyss. Sarah smiled to herself. She knew the guards had to be dead. Nobody could survive a hit that hard. If they did get lucky, they would probably get too exhausted to make it all the way to the shore, and if worse came to worst they were going to be lunch to a squad of sharks.

" I think I killed them ! The boats sank and the 2 guards must have drowned," A proud smile came to Dr. Sanchez's face . " Atta girl, way to get the job down ." The boat began to pick up speed and zoomed across the ocean as fast as it could go . Every so often Dr. Sanchez would look behind him making sure the coast was clear and that they were not being followed.

"Everyone keep on the lookout for Jonathan's laboratory . It should be coming up ahead, " Connor instructed . Dr. Sanchez stared at Connor and looked him deep in the eyes .

"You still havent told me your little plan of yours . What exactly are we going to do at Jonathan's laboratory ?"

"We are going to bomb it ."

" And why may I ask ?"

" Simple. To stop the virus. Once we blow up the lab there's literally no way Jonathan will ever have the chance to make any more of his deadly serums .Meaning he won't have the chance to poison anymore food products and spread the disease, " Connor clarified .

Dr. Sanchez gave this thought. "Last time i checked, we didnt pack a high explosive bomb."

" What I had in mind was to burn the lab by myself. I'm highly capable of doing this alone. You just have to believe in me , I know I can do this ."

The head director respected Connor's choice and didn't say another word. If Connor really wanted to do this then it was up to him ,but he had to know the consequences . There was a high chance he was not going to make it out alive , and a chance he would . It just reflected on how well he would be able to control his powers .

" Ok ,but be careful ," said Dr. Sanchez. "You only have one shot and dont mess it up. The whole world's counting on you . If you blow it were finished."

" I know ," Connor smiled . " I won't let you down."

Chapter 27 : The rise of Dr. Genius

This was it . The last moment of their lives . They would either win or lose, or die hard trying . Connor and his crew of superheroes stood in front of Genius Headquarters the following afternoon . It had been a long ride to get here and there was no turning back . It was still damp outside but most of the rain had stopped . There were a few puddles scattered here and there , and chunks of mud drenched across the grass . Connor took one final deep breath and looked towards the heroes . He had pride in himself that they were going to win and stop Dr .Genius once and for all . Connor knew they didn't have much time though. Though Dr. Genius may still be wounded on that island, there was still a chance he would come back.... to get them !

....

Dr. Genius was trapped under a huge boulder, weak and disoriented he couldn't break free. The boulder had crushed his Ribs and his Collarbone, and was way too heavy to lift. It must have been 3 times his own weight. Dr. Genius was in pain, his calls of help did nothing but echo across the cave. Jonathan was hopeless. He was so mad at himself that he let Connor and his friends get away. He had them ...right in his hands. If He could break free, he would hunt them down and kill them all. But he knew that Connor didn't have to wait for him ...... He would go looking for him. Jonathan took a deep breath and used all his mighty strength to push the boulder off his back. He squatted on his knees, pulling up. The weight was crucifying, it was so heavy his back must have broken. Sweat poured down his face, and his muscles in his body were screaming at him. Jonathan's robotic suit must have been broken because it wasn't doing any good. Jonathan lifted the boulder over his head and dropped it on the ground. Jonathan was relieved, he had broken free and could finally make his escape. Limping away slowly, he made his way out of the cave . Then to his surprise he got a message from his ear phone, it was from General Francis. Jhonatan hit the call button .

" Hello?"

" Is this Jhonatan? "

Jonathan put a hand to his side." Yes ," he rasped out of breath. " I'm alive . I'm ok ."

There was a sigh of relief on the other side of the phone." That's great to hear. Anyway, we know where the heroes are ."

A smile came across Dr. genius's face." Where ?" he spat, blood curling down the side of his chin.

" Genius Headquarters sir."

" Why ? " he questioned . "Why are they there ? "

The voice was quiet for a second. " To blow up the laboratory. They're going to destroy all of the serums ."

Jonathan became furious, he picked up a pile of rocks and threw them across the water. " WE HAVE TO STOP THEM," he bellowed. " WE CANT LET THEM WIN. OTHERWISE ARE 20 YEARS OF WORK WILL BE FINISHED ."

" I understand , sir ," General Francis said quietly.

" Good," Dr. Genius put on his helmet. "I'm coming over and I will finish the kids off by myself. All I want you to do is prevent them from entering the facility ," He put on his rubber gloves. "Understand ? " he said into his earphone.

" Yes , sir ."

" Goodbye , General," Jonathan hung up. He then looked across the waters, contempt in his eyes. Those young heroes wouldn't stop him... they didn't stand a chance.

By the time they had made it inside the laboratory over 100 guards were pronounced dead . Jonathan's troops were highly outnumbered and did not stand a chance against the large group of heroes . So far their plan was working efficiently . They had saved Sarah, got past the entrance of the lab, and had stopped security . There would only be a few more obstacles to face but once they overcame them their mission would be complete .

" Come on guys try to stay together, " Connor whispered quietly .

A few kids in the back were begging to wander around the lab by themselves touching potion bottles and admiring everything they could see.

"This lab is fracking awesome . They've got so much cool stuff ," said Frank."It's like Snape's potion making class from Harry Potter. I wonder which is the Felix Felis. You know, the one that brings good fortune?"

Connor shook his head in disbelief . He really didn't have time for this right now!

" I know this place is cool , I get it ! but we gotta stay focused . Jonathan is still out there and before long he'll be back to get us ."

"Ok ,ok, ok calm down . We're all just trying to have a little fun here,"said Frank .
The heroes continued on their expedition trying to cover as much ground as they could . The laboratory was so huge it took nearly 1 hour for the group to make it up the 10th floor . It was like an Amazon warehouse. Products were being made , and workers worked constantly on creating potions and all sorts of different toxic chemicals . Connor had never been in such a place in his life . He had never seen so many rooms and workers that he was nearly starstruck . Once in a while the group would have to take cover in order to hide themselves , but for the most part ,none of the workers really paid much attention to their appearance . Peering through the glass window , crammed in a huddle, the heroes could see how the chemicals were made. The scientists would use a beaker and squirt a highly dangerous chemical called Neopixels, in which they would put in food products. It was a really fascinating process , but also very

dangerous at the same . Connor took one last look through the window and gathered up the gang . It was go time !

" Alright guys, are we ready ? "

The heroes looked at each other and nodded their heads in agreement .

" Yes ! "

" Yes ."

" Yes !"

They all shouted . Connor smiled and adjusted his mask .

" You guys know the plan . On the count of 3 were all going to run into the lab room and start attacking ! I will use my powers to blast fireballs , and the rest of you will use your abilities to blow up as many samples of the Neopixels as possible ."

Frank , Sarah, and the rest of the group listened closely and got in their ready potions .

" Ok, bring it on ," The heroes all huddled in a circle and put their hands together."On the count of three . 1 .. 2... 3... Assemble ! "

Sarah waved her arms over her head and closed her eyes . She rubbed her fingertips together forming a huge gigantic tidal wave . The students backed up, giving Sarah some space . Sarah looked at Connor and smiled. Connor blushed and gave her the thumbs up . Connor knew Sarah could do it, she just had to believe in herself ! After a couple more deep breaths she was ready . The tidal wave was beginning to get bigger and would soon have the power to break through the door . All of the students watched in amazement as the wave began to spin faster and faster by the second . Before long the wave went up to the ceiling and the water came splurging rapidly towards the glass door . Connor and the rest of the heroes bent down on their knees , trying to cover themselves from the flying glass . Hundreds of guards were startled from their presence as they watched floods of water make their way into the lab !The heroes then submerged into the lab , fists held high and weapons by their sides. The group entered the room like an ant colony, swarms of people filling in. Connor ran up to one of the guards and hit him with a ball of flame. The worker went spurtiling in the air and hit a wall with a deadly crash. Frank was by his side and sweeped one of the other workers off his feet, while Sarah hit the others with strong punches. The rest of the crew were hitting the workers over the head with glass veils and whatever they could find. Connor and his friends had to put in everything they learned in combat training in this situation, that's what it came down to . One of the men from the back of the group came chagrin forward with a spear in his hand . He looked like a Greek god . With his long blonde hair , huge bulky shoulders, and a black helmet hung on his head , he could have idolized Zeus Really well . The kid was clearly good at fighting . He clearly had amazing skills and killed almost everyone in his path .

"Dude ," Frank whispered. " This dude must be from Athens. Isn't he like Hercules or something?"

"No silly," he said as he swung his sword at a guard which was perched in his left hand."My name is the Guardian," He talked in a greek accent, each word bitter and unclear . " I was born in Greece and my father is Odin," He stabbed another ratiner in the chest. "But as you can see I'm kinda busy here , now's not the best time to talk ."

Frank apologized. "Yeah sorry , it's just I've never seen a real Greek good before ."
The battle continued . More scientists and workers began to fall to the ground and more deaths began to rise . So far the heroes had outnumbered the scientists 2 to 1 ! But the battle was still far from over. Connor continued to wound the men with his fire skills, and was getting tired easily after 20 minutes. He didn't know how long he could fight , until he would collapse . Meanwhile, on the other end of the lab Sarah was back on her feat shooting more waves of water out of her hands . Over 10 men were struck by the force knocking them against a nearby wall . Frank was still on the other side of the room fighting against a small group of scientists who were now holding razor sharp wrenches ! Frank dodged their attacks as they tried to stab Frank, but they just were not quick enough . Frank was unstoppable . He was fast, quick, and did not get hit even once . Frank had spent the entire year working on combat training and was ready for whatever came to him . But Just when he was getting tired of dodging more blades ,a large fireball came spinning rapidly towards the small group . The impact was so large that the small group of men were burned alive ! Their faces and hands were charoled , and death defying screams could be heard . Frank backed away from the roaring flames and appeared behind him . Connor was there with his superhero

costume, in shreds , His palms red , his face burning, and was on his knees, screaming at the top of his lungs.The fire quickly spread around the laboratory, making it hard to breath in the thickening rising smoke. All of the doctors seemed to be dead and out conscious, and the whole room was destroyed. Connor had done it . He had blown up the lab and destroyed all of the samples. In the next 20 minutes, the fire would continue to spread and the whole facility would burn. Now, the heroes had to all escape before it was too late.

" We have to get out of here ," Frank coughed. " Now !" His eyes were watering and the smoke was making it hard for him to breathe.

Connor nodded his head .

" Ok . Frank, I want you to round up everyone and lead them towards the 10th floor staircase . Take them down to the 1st first floor and run back to the Academy as fast as you can ."

Frank looked at Connor .

" But what are you going to do ? You can't just stay here by yourself ."

" It's not over Frank . We may have stopped the virus from spreading but Doctor Genius may still be on his way. I have to finish him once and for all... I can't let him live."

 Then a figure stepped out of the crowd. It was Sarah. She walked up to Connor.

" Please ," she begged. " Don't leave - I wouldn't stand it if you died."

Connor stroked Sarahs hair gently. " It's ok ," he said soothingly."It's ok ."

 " But what if everything doesn't work out?" Sarah asked gently . "What if I never get to see you again . If something happened to you I couldn't live with the pain Connor!"

Connor smiled. " I promise you , il c'mon back. I won't let you down ."

Sarah looked up at Connor, tears filling her eyes. " I love you Connor, " she managed, the words struggling to come out from the smoke. " I love you too," Connor said back. The 2 then stared into each other's eyes admirably, then kissed. Connor then let go . He looked back at Sarah and began to tear up. He tried holding back the tears , but the pain was too much to bear . How could he stand losing Sarah? How would he stand losing every one he loved? Connor put that thought aside and tried to stay determined and focused. I can do this , he thought. Tomorrow I'll be with my friends at the pool and having a good time, everything will be ok , he told himself. Then the heroes gathered up and gave Connor fist bumps and playful slaps.

" Good luck buddy," Nightwing said .

" Yeah, we believe in you," the Guardian chimed in .

Connor had never felt so much comfort in his life . He wiped away the tears and stood proudly . Sarah emerged from his arms and went back to the group.

" Don't worry guys, I'll defeat him ..... Before long I'll be back at the Heroes Academy safe and sound . I've been training a lot in the past couple of months and I think I'm ready to show the world who I really am . I Am not afraid of dying.. If I die to stop Mcdell, then it's worth dying for. At Least then I know that I truly am a hero ."

Frank smiled and put a hand on Connor's shoulder . " I believe in you . Now Go catch em tiger . You got a job to do ."

....

The fire began to spread . Over half of the laboratory was already in ruins, and all of the serums were destroyed. Connor stood alone waiting for the mad scientists to return . It had been over 20 minutes since the other heroes had left and Connor was begging to get impatient . Just when Connor was about to give up, a man in a robotic suit entered the laboratory . He had an angry scowl on his face and large boots that crushed the ground beneath him . From the look of it, Connor knew it was Dr. Genius .

" How are you even alive?" Connor managed."You're supposed to be dead!"

The mad man slipped out a disturbing chuckle . His veins were sticking out of his neck and his face was red.

" It's so nice to see you, Connor . It feels like forever since we last talked to each other ."

Connor clenched his fists and walked closer to Jonathan . Before he could react ,the mad scientist grabbed the boy by the hand and leaned him in closer . He studied Connor carefully and plucked his childish hair .

" What a beautiful little child you are... Why do you look so scared, " he said gently . " I'm not going to bite ."

Connor let go of his grip from him. "You should be the scared one Jhonathan. All your lifetime's work is gone. I destroyed your samples. The virus is over. I won Jhonathan , and you lost."

Jhonatah chuckled. " You think you're so smart huh ?" He fished a green bottle out of a small compartment in his suit . " Well ,what you didn't know was that I had one more sample. All i have to do is launch this in my machine, and tada! The virus will continue. It may not last forever but it will kill thousands of more people."

Connor stumbled back in surprise. If what Dr. Genius was saying was true then there really would be no way to stop the virus !

" No... No .... You-you can't do this !" Connor shouted angrily , his face beginning to turn red .

" Oh, but I can," Dr. Genius said . "Once I launch this sample there will be no way for you or your little gang of superheroes to stop me ! I'll be unstoppable, I'll destroy the world, and finally get back what this world has taken from me !" the scientists demanded happily .

Connor held his hands up in surrender . "Let's sort this out, Jonathan . Just you and me. If I win , you give me the sample. If I lose, you keep it ."

Jonathan snickered."Sounds fair , but I'm warning you , you're messing with the wrong guy ."

The 2 arch enemies walked towards each other . They moved around in a circle like a pack of hungry lions. Connor made the first move. He swung a punch at Dr. Geniuses head , leaving him dizzy and unstable. Connor swung again punching him in the chest, his knuckles bleeding. Jonatahn expected the punches like it was nothing and just smiled . Connor got angrier by the second . He hated seeing Jonathan look so happy and proud. This crazy man had kidnapped his best friend, almost killed him, and was creating a deadly virus that was killing millions of people . Connor wanted nothing more than to see him suffer and die ! As time flew by, each of the young heroes' punches began to get stronger and stronger to the point where Connor could hardly breathe . Left , right, uppercut, down, bodyblow, these were the motions Connor repeated over and over again. Then when Connor was least expecting a hit, a huge metal arm punched him in the gut, sending him flying across the room. Connor hit a table, and tumbled to the ground , the air knocked out of him. Connor lay there motionless, the pain taking over his body . Connor tried to get up but kept falling down. Then, Dr. Genius stormed up to Connor and picked him up by the neck. Connor kicked and screamed but nothing helped. Connor was lifted off his feet and into the air. Dr. Genius began punching Connor in the face continuously, blood streaming down Connor's skulp. Connor tried catching his breath but the pain was holding him back . In Connors mind he knew he had broken almost everything in his body . His Rib was broken from the cave fight, his Arm was dislocated, and now his Jaw was broken . Connor wished all of the pain would go away. He wished the fighting would be over . But most importantly he wished Dr. Genius was dead ! Back at the cave Connor had a chance to defeat Jonathan. He wished he could have just killed him there . Dr. Genius gripped harder on Connors neck, making it impossible for Connor to breathe. He then threw him into a window, glass shattering down on him . Connors' lip was now busted and bruised and pieces of glass were stuck into his skin . The hero limped on his right leg and into the open hall . The fire was spreading and the smoke was getting toxic . It would only be a matter of time before the building would collapse and Connor would be dead . Connor had to make the fight quick if he wanted to make it out alive.

" Davidson !!! WHERE ARE YOU GOING ?" an angry voice yelled from inside the lab .

Connor continued through the halls, coughing and his eyes watering. He proceeded to a narrow staircase and caught his breath. Dr. Genius was begging to make his way towards Connor angrier than ever .

" You can't hide from me ! "

Connor put his hands up for protection but the madman's two large robotic hands tossed the boy over his back . Connor squirmed and began to throw consecutive punches at Dr. geniuses robotic suit, but it was useless . Dr. Genius lifted Connor over his head and threw him over the balcony. Connor waved his hands in desperation attempting to grab onto something but it was already too late . Connor was gaining so much speed that by the time he could even think of a plan ,he came crashing down to the ground . He rolled down the stairs , his hands shielding his face , and his body rolled in a ball. He must have rolled down 2 staircases because when he came down to the first floor, he was all bruised up and wounded. The back of his head had a gnarly gash , and his leg was in so much pain it was hard to walk on. He must have sprained it. Connor slowly got onto his knees and rubbed his fingertips together . With as much force as possible Connor released 3 sets of fireballs each the size of a basketball . He looked towards the top of the staircase where he spotted Jonathan . He moved his arms towards his target and released the massive sets of flames . The fireballs went in three separate directions and then came crashing into the top staircase. Bricks went flying everywhere , fire began to erupt, soon causing Jonathan to go tumbling down a sideway staircase. He rolled down in a fast motion that caused pieces of his robotic suit to come splurging off his body . He hit the ground just before a large boulder of bricks smashed into his chest . Dr. Genius was down ! Connor got back onto his knees and slowly crept towards Jonathan. He did not seem to be moving , and he looked motionless . The young hero lifted a small pile of bricks off the enemies chest and looked into Dr. Genius' eyes . Everything seemed normal , and for once Connor thought the battle was over . But before he could celebrate Connor stumbled back when he noticed that the madman's were wide open and a smile was perched on his face . Connor had jumped to conclusions. Dr. Genius really wasn't dead after all . In Fact he looked desperate for revenge ! Connors' back hit against a nearby wall as he tried to digest the information . There was no way Jonathan was still possibly alive ! He had fallen down the stairs, was hit by bricks, and struck by destructive fireballs. Connor took a small breath still in a stage of panic , but then before long cast a new set of fireballs to come shooting out of his mouth ! Connor could feel the heat of his tongue rise and could feel the force of gravity working against him . Connor pushed with all his might and let out the flames . The wave of heat spun in a small circle and came smashing into Jonathan sending his entire suit to be covered in roaring flames. The scientist screamed and peered down at the fire . He tried to get the flames off him but things were just getting worse .

Connor was enjoying the moment . For once he actually was holding up a fight and had a chance to defeat the enemy. If Connor could continue to set attacks on Dr. Genius then before long he would be dead . But the young hero couldn't celebrate now . There was still a fight and no one had won just yet …

" Give up Jonathan ! surrender and I'll leave you in peace ."

Dr. Genius' eyes lit up as the fire spread rapidly onto his arms .

" I will never surrender to my enemies . Your nothing but a small child with a stupid cape and costume . I'm stronger than you , now accept it !"

Connor looked down at the veil by his side. He had to find a way to distract him and steal it. The scientist met Connors eyes and his expression lowered .

" I see…. You're thinking up a plan aren't you? "

Connor gulped trying to act normal . Dr. Genius couldnt find out .

" Im …im… - im not thinking up anything," he said in a non convincing tone.

Dr. Genius pushed a small button on the end of his suit and stepped out . He wore a long white lab coat with yellow rubber gloves. He looked small and fragile, and his face was all wrinkly and old. Up close, he looked like Einstein. Except for the fact that he wasn't helping humanity, he was destroying it. Dr. Genius looked at Connor and back at the veil on the floor. He knew what Connor was planning and he had to stop him. Connor slid on the floor baseball style, and grabbed hold of the veil. Dr. Genius tried to grab it first, but Connor already had it. Connor slid it in his pocket, and got back on his feet. Dr. Genius was angry .

"Give it to me boy," he warned. "Give it back."

" Oh you want this," Connor taunted, holding the veil in his hand."Then go fetch!"

Connor threw the bottle in the air. The bottle went spinning and before Jonathan could catch it , dropped to the floor in hundreds of pieces.

" Noooo!!" he screamed. "That- that was the last one ,"Connor smiled."I guess you lose Jonathan. The virus is over, your plan failed. And now it's time to die ! "

Dr. Genius stormed up to Connor in frustration. But Connor was already expecting this. Connor leaped up into the air , as a fist came so close to his body that Connor was nearly hit. Connor dogged the strike in middle air performing a frontflip , and then landed on his 2 feet. Dr. Genius swiped at the open air as Connor disappeared from sight . The hero then jumped onto Jonathan's back when he wasn't looking and began to strangle him . He wrapped his hands around the scientist's neck and squeezed as hard as he could , giving no sign of mercy . Connor tugged harder, until Dr. Geniuses face was littarley blue. Connor then rolled off his back and swiped him off his feet, and the mad scientist tumbled to the ground in agony . Jonathan was still for a moment which meant Connor had another chance to strike ! Without hesitation the young hero released a ball of flame that went straight towards Dr. Geniuses head ! The burning flames flickered fast as they struck the scientist's hair. Jonathan let out a death defying scream as he felt the heat rise up his neck . Connor smiled to himself, admiring his handiwork.

" Hey Jonathan?" Connor began .

Dr. Genius turned towards the speaking boy.

 "You know your hair looks really nice !"

" AHHH ! " the mad scientist screamed, trying to put out the flames. "You little peasant."

" You look pretty hot there, and it looks like you need to cool down."

" That's it boy."

" Catch me if you can ."

Connor ran down another hallway as fast as he could . He looked beside him once in a while making sure Jonathan wasn't creeping up behind him . Connor passed over 10 different rooms and work offices ,and his mind was spinning like crazy . He felt like he was wandering in some sort of labyrinth. Connor proceeded through a dark hallway , the smoke filling his lungs. Conor could hear Doctor Genius trotting behind him, his evil laugh echoing across the halls. Connor looked at a glass panel and could see Dr. Genius' reflection from behind. He was a tall murky shadow with his hair in a blaze. Connor continued his route, his hands clutching his ribs, and his arm twisted in a weird angle. His fizzion was foggy and it was hard to make sense of his surroundings. Connor was damp and hot, so he pulled off his rubber mask off his head and put it in his pocket. Dr. Genius was only a few feet away from him and he didn't look good. His whole face was burned and his skin looked like it may peel off. Connor closed his eyes and a huge flame , the size of a baseball floated in his hands. He used all his strength to throw it across the room, it hit Dr. Genius square in the chest. The scientist dropped to the ground, screaming and cursing at the top of his lunges. Connor knew that without his robotic suit, he didn't stand a chance. Connor continued to release fire balls and all his strength seemed to be wearing him out. Connor thenused all his guts to walk up to Dr. Genius and meet him face to face. Connor wasn't going to run any more, he wasn't afraid of him. He had to face this man , and make him pay. Connor went over to a glass box and punched through the glass. His knuckles were bleeding, and he had a bad cut on his hand. Connor, fighting the pain, picked up the Ax which was displayed in the box and held it by his side. The Ax was heavy and took all his strength to lift it up. Connor lifted the Ax over his head and stared at the madman, who was startled and scared.

" This is it ," said Connor. "This is where it ends ."

Dr. Genius looked up at Connor, his face all black and crumpled. " You've ruined everything boy, but it doesnt give me the discipline to not give up. I will not surrender to you under the name of god, even if you shall kill me. I have lived for a purpose, a purpose that has been a good cause ," The words were struggling to come out, each word bitter and unclear. Connor knew he was dying, he didn't have long to live. "For eons I have been known as a hero, a hero that has served his country well. I have proved to humanity that whatever kills me makes me stronger. I am indeed a mad scientist, a really mad one. But you must remember that what I was doing was also good."

" No ,"Connor shouted."You never were good."

Dr. Genius smiled, his rotten jibs sticking out. "As a young boy Things never were easy. Dad died when I was 8, mom left because of a felony, my brother overdosed. You don't understand what the world has given us. We have to be judged by our race, religion , and choices. But imagine a world where everything is free. Food, houses, health care, it would be the dream of a lifetime. No more bullying or discrimination, like i was given. My only other way to show my true self, was creating this virus. Killing thousands would help millions. With the virus going around, all across the country people are donating . With this money we can build a structured community where we can be free."

" That's wrong," Connor said startledly. "That plan will never work. You're a scientist for crying out loud . Shouldn't you be helping the environment, not destroying it."

Dr. Genius chuckled."Every scientist has a hypothesis , Connor . And my hypothesis is that I'm right. For decades I have helped society, I have created so many inventions. For god's sake , who invented the microwavable fridge? or the everlasting water ridge in africa? Well , that was me. So you see, you may think I'm bad for causing this virus, but I'm doing it for a reason , a very good reason. Every year people get sick. Whether it's the flu , or chickenpox. Soon, this virus will go down in history, and will be remembered for eons. And I ...will be the cause."

Connor couldn't believe what he had just heard. This man was insane!

" Kill me," Dr. Genius flared."Kill me."

Connor was still and silent. He stopped walking , and his heart began to race.

"I know you don't have it in you . You're just a lonely scared little boy."

Adrenaline pumped in Connors blood stream. His palms were sweaty and he was scared. He didn't know what to do. Should he kill him, or let him live. This was too overwhelming. Connor dropped the ax to the ground, and walked away. That was his final decision! He wasnt a murder. He would neevr be.

" I knew you didn't have it in you ," Dr. Genius called to him . " You're not a hero. You're a zero ."

Connor ignored the shouting curses, as he proceeded down the hall. He knew either way Dr. Genius was dying, it didn't make a difference if he killed him or not. With the smoke rising and the flames growing bigger, Connor ran out of the building and away from the facility. The last thing he remembered was the explosion of the building , and the distinct screaming of a mad scientist.

Chapter 28: The hospital

" Connor ? "

" Wake up !"

Connor opened his eyes slowly. He was dazed and confused, and awoke in boxer shorts and a white t-shirt. He must have been in the hospital, because there was a mechanical ventilator with plastic tubes in his arms, and a doctor standing over him.

" Where am I ?" Connor managed.

The doctor came up to connor. " You're in the medical wing . You fractured your rib cage, tore your lcu, sprained your ankle, had a mild concussion, and broke your wrist."

Connor sat up on his pillow. "How- how did this happen?" he asked.

The doctor looked through a pile of papers.

" Well, according to the paperwork it looks like you got into a fight."

Connor shifted his position on the bed, and tried to remember what had happened . Everything was a blur to him.

" Will I be ok?" Connor asked out of the ordinary ."I mean, do you think I'll be able to continue my training ? "

The doctor glanced at Connor through his round spectacles. "You need rest. Looking at your report, it looks like you're going to need 2 weeks of a break ."

" 2 weeks ! I -I- can't stay here that long . I need to stop Dr. Genius and - ."

" He's dead ."

Connor gasped. How could this be true ?

" You probably don't remember much due to your concussion, but he was burned alive . Genius Headquarters caught on fire and his body went down with it."

" So that's it then ?.... he's gone .... i - i defeated him?" Connor questioned .

" Yep , you're all over the Metropolis Daily News. Superman was even kind enough to write a review ."

Connors jaw dropped. "So the virus is over now right ?"

The doctor nodded. " if you've seen the news , you would've known that everything is back to normal. The death of Dr. Genius spread all across the world like a wildfire, and the cases of deaths have gone down."

A huge weight was lifted off Connors shoulders. He took a heavy deep breath and sighed in relief . It was over . He really had saved the day afterall .

" How about my friends ? are-are- Sarah and Frank OK?" he stammered .

The doctor smiled. "Actually they're fine . They came to stop by Yesterday and brought you some flowers and chocolates." The Doctor pointed to a small nightstand where notecards and beautiful flowers were displayed .

Connor jumped up from his position .

" Wait, how long have I been asleep?"

The doctor put a hand on Connor's shoulder and gently pushed him back down .

" 1 week ."

" you were in a coma. It wasn't serious but we didn't know if you would wake up."

Connor looked up at the doctor. He had a brown mustache and a black beard. " That felt good."

" what ?"

" Your touch."

"oh, I forgot to mention. I'm related to Doctor Strange and my power is to heal people."

Connor smiled . "well, thank you .... I feel much better ."

The Doctor showed his hand like he was swatting a fly .

"Dont worry about it."

Connor laid his head back on his pillow. He closed his eyes and doozed of to sleep.

Chapter 29: The morning report

Sydney Rodriguez stepped up to the podium and adjusted her buttoned skirt. She took a deep breath and grabbed a hold onto a wireless microphone . The producer crew adjusted their cameras and gave the thumbs up signal . They were live ! Over 100 million people were watching the News . They all were enjoying big breakfasts and waiting for the local Sunday report . In the past couple of months the news was filled with nothing but reports about the virus and rising cases . But today was different . Today Sydney had a brand new story to tell. A good one .

" Good morning America my name is Sydney Rodriguez and welcome back to Cnn news . Today I'm here at county lane hospital reporting live from 39th street ." The young women pointed towards a large white bricked hospital where over hundreds of people were walking in and out .

" I'm so excited to report that cases of the new virus have been decreasing strinomlily … Over 10,000 people have been released from the hospital today with no more signs of sickness ."

The reporter took a small breath and then proceeded on .

"   More worldwide restaurants are starting to open again , shops no longer have strict guidelines, and masks are no longer needed ! From the looks of things it looks like everything is returning back to normal ,"Sydney protested happily .

On the other end of the television screams of joy and relief could be heard . Men and women jumped up from their chairs and twirled around with pleasure . After being in quarantine for over a year and hardly seeing the outside world, life was returning to its normal standards .

" Can you believe it, Martha ?" An old man said as he sipped his morning coffee . " It really is over ! "
The old cheerful lady hugged her husband and smiled . " I can't believe it . We can finally move on from this terrible crisis ! "

Sydeny rodiguez gave a warm smile and said her final words . " Well that's right folks, Virus Kilo18 has finally been put to a stop . From now on enjoy the beautiful weather and start living your life again . This is Sydney Rodriguez signing off ." The lights dimmed , the network concluded, and then everything went black .

Chapter 30: The ceremony

Connor awoke the next day with a sore neck and a headache . His mouth was dry and his breath smelled like rotten garbage . Of course he had fallen asleep and before he knew it a new day had begun . A knock on the door startled Connor from his presence . It was loud and sounded furious . Connor sat himself up into a comfortable position and told the guest to come in . The door creaked open slowly and a young girl stepped into the dim light . She had blond hair and was wearing a beautiful red skirt . Connor squinted his eyes and recognized that it was Sarah ! She looked so beautiful that it was hard for Connor to tell that it was even her .

" Sarah.. Is- is that you ? " he questioned , his voice echoing across the room .

The girl took a seat next to Connor and put her hand into his . She looked at him closely and let out a proud smile .

" Yeah Connor it's me ! "

Connor blushed a little as he felt her hand touch his . He was so glad that she had come to see him .

" But - but Sarah, what are you doing here ? Don't you have classes today?"

Sarah let out a chuckle if she just had heard some funny joke .

“ No, haven't you heard ? Dr. Sanchez has decided to cancel classes this week . He said he wanted to give the school a few days of rest .... You know .... Because of the battle and -.”

Connor cutted her off and nodded his head . “ Yeah, I know , “ he interrupted .

Sarah whipped back her hair and adjusted on some lipstick . Connor still had a lot of questions .

“ Why are you dressed up ? Is there some sort of party or dance going on today ? “ Connor said .
“ That's the reason why I came here, “ Sarah began . “ I wanted to let you know that this evening there's going to be a huge ceremony .... Dr. Sanchez said he would like it if you came .”

Connor looked deeply into Sarah's blue eyes . “ A ceremony ? “ he asked curiously .

Sarah nodded her head . “ Yeah , the whole school is going to be there ... Dr. Sanchez will be giving out some trophies and prizes for a few lucky heroes .”

Connors' heart began to beat . He gave Sarah a warm smile .

“ That sounds amazing ! But ... ,“ Connor stopped and lowered his expression . “I can't go ... I mean, look at me . Everyone will probably just make fun of me because of how awful I look .”

Sarah grabbed Connor by the chin and looked at him hard . She wasn't going to put up with his attitude .

“ Connor James Davidson, you are one of the most handsomest boys I've ever seen .... Don't doubt yourself . You saved the world from an evil scientist for good sakes and you're worried about your appearance ? I'm sure everyone here wouldn't mind if you came by ,“ she said gently .

Connors face began to brighten up . He was so glad he had a friend that actually stood up for him .

“ Thanks ... I'll be there .”

The 2 shared a warm hug. Connor could feel the warmth and comfort and he didn't dare to let go . Ever since Connor had first arrived at Heroes Academy Sarah was always there for him . She'd help him with his homework, she'd always stop by to check on him , and most importantly she was always there when Connor needed her most .

By 7:00 pm almost the entire school had entered the gymnasium . Students were crammed inside the building sharing laughs with one another while eating apitzers . Dr. Sanchez entered the gym 5 after 7 with a stack of his papers in his hand and a box of metal trophies . Connor was sitting in the front of the room with a nicely dressed tuxedo and black shiny shoes . He had cleaned himself up earlier and he looked nice and presentable . Sarah and Frank were sitting beside Connor with proud smiling faces . The ceremony was about to begin ! Dr. Sanchez walked up towards the stage where a microphone stand was displayed . The headmaster slicked back his hair and tapped the microphone with his palm .

" Attention heroes, can we please quiet down ?"

The shouting went down instantly. The room was silent.

" Tonight I would like to present a set of trophies to a few fine young heroes."

Everyone in the room gazed around the room wondering what students Dr. Sanchez was going to mention . Deep down inside Connor knew he was most likely going to be picked . Sarah and Frank shared a similar thought .

" Last week we experienced a tragic incident... A mad scientist named Dr. Genius kidnapped one of are students, almost killing her."

 Sarah tried to hide her expression.

"Because of all of you brave heroes we were able to rescue her ... If it wasn't for all your courage, bravery, and strength we never would have done it ."

 Cheerful claps echoed across the room as well as faint whistling noises .
Dr. Sanchez smiled and then continued on with his speech .

" However , 3 students in this room were brave enough to take down the
impossible …. I'd like to congratulate Sarah , Frank , and the brave and
magnificent Connor Davidson !! "

More applause.

" But the true hero out of the 3 would have to be Connor . If it wasn't for
him, Dr. Genius would still be alive." Connor smiled. "Connor had the guts
to face him and stop him once in for all , even if he knew the
consequences. Connor has proved himself as being a loyal hero and shall
be remembered in the school's hall of fame ."

Louder applause.

" Now step right up and get your trophies ! "

The heroes shared a look with one another and together proceeded up a
small set of stairs . They waved at all of the students and posed for a few
snapping photographs . Connor felt like he was some sort of celebratory
living in a dream . He had never seen so many people so proud of him .
Dr. Sanchez tapped the heroes on the backs and gave them a gentle
squeeze. There was a huge line , which moved very slowly. Most of the kids
just got average sized trophies, but Sarah and Frank got bigger ones . To
Connors surprise , he received a trophy so big and heavy that he could
hardly hold it . On the trophy a set of inspirational words were carved in ,

and a picture of a superhero was planted in the middle.   . Connor raised
the trophy high in the air and even more applause was made . For once
Connor felt like a true hero. Not a zero .

Chapter 31: Final goodbye

The sun was shining and the air was thick and crisp. The Birds were chirping , the sky was a shade of pink, and it looked like it was going to be a beautiful day. Connor and Sarah had rented out a canoe and decided to spend the day fishing . In the past week they had encountered so much drama that they just wanted to relax and lay low . You know... have fun for once. It was the last day of the school year . Connors first year had gone by so fast he could hardly remember it . Just over 6 months ago Connor was nothing but a bored child locked up in his room . And 183 days later he was fighting to save the world . It was all too much for Connor to process . He still could hardly believe that he was a real life superhero . All his life he read comic books, and saw the movies, and dreamt of being a hero. But being a real one wasn't that easy. Being a hero meant you had to take the hits and punches and keep moving forward, even if it's tough and you lose people through the way. Connor had lost many people in the battle at the cave . He'd almost got burned alive in a laboratory, and was minutes away from being killed by a mad scientist, but that didn't stop his bravery and courage . Deep inside Connor knew this was just the beginning . This was the beginning of a battle that would take decades to win. But Connor knew he would need his friends by his side. They were the most important. Connor still had many questions that weren't answered , but those had to wait. Maybe when he was older he would find out for himself.

" Hey you ok?"

Connor gleamed at the still water . " Yeah," he said quietly. " I'm fine."

Sarah placed her hand into Connors . "You know you can talk to me right ? if something is on your mind you can tell me ."

Connor threw a pebble into the pond, the water making a ripple. " Yeah I know," he mumbled under his breath. There were so many things on Connors mind he could hardly think . Eventually Connor would have to tell Sarah what was really going on .

" Sarah,I'm not sure if I'll be able to come back ." He put down his head in disgrace .

Sarah was starstruck for a moment . The 2 of them didn't communicate for a good 30 seconds . All you could hear was the still water and the echoing of birds .

" Oh... Why- why not ?" she asked calmly .

Connor put his hands on his face and looked Sarah in the eye .

" Well, you know . I still have regular school to finish up and my parents are probably worried sick about me. I also need a break. I want to enjoy the last few months of July and hang out with my friends. "

Sarah looked concerned.

" Don't take it personally. I mean you and Frank are great friends and all, but I also want to-."

" Hang out with normal people ," she interrupted .

" Yeah ."

" I get it."

Sarah nodded her head . This was so much for her to process . " Do you think youll ever come back ? "

Connor couldn't bring himself to answer this question . " I'll think about it … For now I think I just want to live my life . No crime. No pressure. Just lay low ."

Sarah stroked back a strand of hair. " I wish I had a family."

Connor was heartbroken by this comment, He locked his eyes into Sarahs and put a hand on her shoulder. He felt Really bad for her. " You can come with me if youd -."
He was cut short . " I'm sorry, Connor, i - i can't ." There was a long pause . "I…. I have to stay here . This is where I belong ."

 Connor nodded his head . It was hard to accept the reality . " I'm sorry, Sarah, about everything. You were so young."

Sarah squinted at the sun. "I know my parents are in a better place. They're probably looking down at me and telling me how proud they are."

Connor smiled. " You know, your parents ….They were lucky to have someone like you ."

Sarah began to tear up. Her eyes got puffy and dry.

" I love you, Connor ," Sarah laid her head on his shoulder. " You're the best person I've ever met . And I mean it ."

Connor brought his lips to hers and they kissed. Connor felt so relaxed and comfortable, and didn't dare to let go. For once he felt like he wanted to stay . He dreamed of kissing in the warm sunlight, soaking in the pool , and exploring the campus . But deep in his heart he knew he couldn't. He had to go home, even if it meant having to wait a whole 6 months. He wouldn't leave Sarah, he would return next year.
Connor let go and pushed Sarah in closer.

" Sarah, I'll come back for you … I promise, " he said on the urge of tears .

Sarah chuckled. She looked Connor deep in the eyes and smiled .

  " I'll be waiting, " she said .

Connor took a deep breath and wiped a tear from eye . Though it was hard to face the truth, Connor just smiled . Deep in his heart he knew he would see Sarah again ,and that his story was just beginning .

The End

Authors note :

We want to thank everyone in our family for making this book possible .If it was not for them this book would never have been a success.We also want to dedicate this book to our 6th grade literature teacher Ms. Borah who taught us how to write.